Prologue

Welcome. We don't get many humans here.

Spirits and spectres, yes. But humans must be in an exceptionally precarious and unstable state to find their way to Gloaming Lane.

The lane is at the very edge of the otherworld, after all – a handful of stores and businesses in a forgotten place, home only to outcasts like myself.

Oh, of course – I neglected to introduce myself. I am Kogetsu, proprietor of the Amberglow Candy Store. It is a pleasure to make your acquaintance.

In any case, if you have found your way here, something must be troubling you. Deeply enough to cast your very existence into doubt.

How can I tell? Call it intuition.

Have you found a confection that takes your fancy? Excellent. Allow me to wrap it for you at the counter – this way, please.

No, no – pardon me, but I must insist that you

refrain from peeking into our rear storeroom. What was on the shelves in that large cabinet, you ask? I couldn't possibly comment. After all, curiosity did kill the cat.

Here are your sweets. Be sure to enjoy them in the recommended manner . . . and at the recommended dosage.

Our wares can have unforeseen effects, and we take no responsibility for any event arising from their consumption. *Caveat emptor*, as they say . . .

CHAPTER I

Craving-More Konpeito

I missed my boyfriend.

He hardly ever texted or called me anymore. I knew it wasn't his fault he had so little time for me. He was busy studying for his college entrance exams. But I was still lonely.

When he'd told me he wouldn't have much free time before the big exams, I'd dutifully assured him it was all right, playing the perfectly understanding girlfriend – but I hadn't realized there would be practice exams every single month.

'At least you *have* a boyfriend,' my friends would tell me. 'You should count your blessings.' They didn't understand at all.

My boyfriend was one year ahead of me in school. I'd had a crush on him since junior high, where he was president of the student council. He was so cool and so smart, but always friendly and kind to those around him. I was smitten.

I studied myself half to death to get into the same high school as him, but for most of my first year there, all I could do was admire him from afar. When I finally worked up the courage to ask him out, he said yes. Me, a completely average person, not especially beautiful or brainy, dating someone as perfect as him! It was like a miracle.

But the honeymoon only lasted until spring break. Once he started his third year of high school, he had to buckle down and study for college entrance exams.

Weekend dates were a thing of the past. We didn't even walk to and from school together anymore, because he was always either at cram school or in the study rooms revising.

We were still an item, of course, which should have been better than pining for him from afar. But the truth is, I was more anxious than ever.

I didn't want him to get sick of my selfishness. I didn't want him to decide I was too much of a hassle and break up with me.

But I did want to see him. I wanted to hear

his voice. I wanted him to show more affection.

Was I asking too much? Should I just grin and bear it until his exams were over? But it was only May. Ten more months of this would be torture.

Plus, when he started college, the distance between us would only widen. What if he met another girl in a school club or part-time job, and lost interest in me? What if I spent a whole year waiting patiently, and then we just drifted apart? The thought was unbearable.

But what could I do about it? It wasn't like I could magically redirect his attention my way.

So I did the next best thing: one day after school, I went to pray at the shrine.

It was old and weathered, hidden among the trees on a small hill at the edge of town. I had gone there to pray for luck before my high-school entrance exams and before asking my boyfriend out, and things had worked out for me both of those times, so now I went whenever I had something important coming up. Only in secret, though – I didn't want people to think I was weird for asking the kami for help all the time.

Fortunately, once you climbed the stone staircase

up the hill and stepped into the tree-lined shrine precincts, no one outside could tell you were there.

I tossed my coins into the box, rang the rusty bell, and put my hands together to pray.

May my boyfriend and I stay together forever. May our relationship get closer and stronger.

But even as I prayed, dark thoughts were rising within me.

What if my boyfriend was only with me now because he couldn't be bothered to dump me? What if he'd only agreed to be my boyfriend in the first place on a whim?

What proof did I have that he even truly liked me?

Hot tears stung my eyes.

I knew I was overthinking it. I was on my way to becoming one of those annoying, clingy girls the magazines say boys hate. But he was the first boyfriend I'd ever had. How was I supposed to get everything right when I had no experience to draw on?

It was during this crisis of confidence that I noticed an unusual fragrance in the breeze. I couldn't quite place it, but it was strangely appealing, like a fond memory. I glanced towards the rear of the shrine precinct, where the breeze was coming from, and my eyes widened in surprise.

Beyond the wooden shrine itself, among the row of trees surrounding the precinct, there was a gap. A passageway into the forest.

Had a shrine priest done some pruning? But why only there?

I was sure the fragrance was coming from the opening. It was a mysterious smell, like incense, or old timber.

Gripping my schoolbag tightly, I walked around the shrine towards the opening. Once I got close enough, I saw something even more surprising beyond it: a long, unpaved road lined with retro-looking stores. The stores were all made of wood and hung with round paper lanterns in red and white, like the kind you see at festivals. The setting sun lent the whole scene a warm orange tone.

'But . . . why?' I murmured to myself.

Had this shopping street always been back here? Why did it end at the shrine instead of the main road? It was as if the shrine itself was the gateway.

Something seemed off about the street, but it

was also oddly familiar, like the kind of streetscape you see in old films. In the end my curiosity won out, and I walked through the opening.

The surface under my well-worn loafers wasn't asphalt, but more like compressed sand, with pebbles here and there. Did it even count as a 'street'?

The buildings were old and run-down, and none of the stores were open. Some had signs in their windows reading CLOSED. Others had been slammed shut as soon as I stepped through the gap in the trees. That was a little rude, to be honest.

It was impossible to tell from the outside what most of the stores actually sold. And some of the signs were written in eerie characters I didn't recognize at all. There were no streetlights, and the dangling paper lanterns had a strange unreality about them that gave me goosebumps.

Still, I kept walking. I couldn't even tell you why. Maybe all that brooding over my troubles had left me in a reckless, self-destructive mood. What's odd is that I was normally the first to chicken out of things like this. I couldn't even go inside the makeshift haunted houses some classes ran at the school festival. If my boyfriend had been with me,

I probably would have clung to his arm and begged to turn back.

The street ended at a T-junction, and that was where I finally found a store that looked open, with light spilling from inside. It was the very last building on the street, and made of rich, caramel-brown timber, as old as its neighbours but kept in much better shape. The carved wooden door had a window set in it, and beside it was a pink paper lantern held up on a tall stand.

The handwritten sign read AMBERGLOW CANDY STORE.

Amberglow?

The days of operation were strange, too: 'Closed when the moon is new or full.'

Still, if it was just a candy store, I probably wouldn't get pressured into buying something I couldn't afford. And I was in the mood for something sweet.

I pushed at the door. It opened with a creak, revealing the store's gloomy interior.

A lantern hanging from the ceiling illuminated a haphazard collection of waist-high tables on which the store's wares were arranged. The stock was a strange mixture of timeless, traditional Japanese sweets like *daifuku* and *manju* and modern-but-retro confections like *konpeito*, Kintaro candy and caramels.

'Welcome,' a voice said, making me jump. 'We don't get many humans here.'

I peered into the gloom and saw a man dressed in a kimono and *hakama* trousers standing at the back of the store. He was, in a word, hot. He had a pale complexion, with blond hair a little too long to be called short, and narrow golden eyes. I got the impression he wasn't from around here. His age was hard to guess, too – maybe mid-twenties?

And, just for a moment, I thought I caught a glimpse of two fox-like ears with pale brown fur on top of his head. Probably a trick of the light . . .

'Hello,' I said cautiously. 'What do you mean, you don't get many humans here?'

The corners of his mouth turned up in an insincere smile, making him look less like a real person than a skilfully painted doll.

'Gloaming Lane is located in the gap between your world and the otherworld. The only beings who come here are spirits, spectres, and humans in a precarious and unstable state. Like you, if I may.'

I was a little alarmed by this spiel at first, but then I realized what was happening.

This was some kind of concept store. This other-world stuff was the backstory, and he was playing a character, like an employee at a theme park.

I knew that high-concept cafés and restaurants were popular these days. But it was hard to imagine this place getting much traction hidden away behind a shrine.

'My apologies,' the man continued. His voice was high for a man's, with a cool edge to it. 'I failed to introduce myself. I am Kogetsu, the owner of this establishment.' He offered a polite half-bow.

'Right,' I said slowly. 'So . . . you're a fox or something?'

I figured those fox ears I'd glimpsed earlier had to be some kind of cosplay prop. Maybe I was his first customer in ages, and he was pulling out all the stops for me. It felt cruel not to at least acknowledge his efforts.

'Very perceptive,' Kogetsu said. 'But only half correct.'

'How so?'

Kogetsu just smiled. But since I had him talking about the store's concept, I decided to try asking about the days of operation, too.

'Why are you closed on the new and full moon?' I asked.

'I dislike them,' he said. 'I am a creature of the in-between. When the strength of the moon's influence is at either extreme, I find it difficult to bear.'

He sounded almost bitter. Maybe it was something to do with his 'half-fox' backstory? But I also didn't see any other employees around. Was he running this place alone, with only two days off a month? I'd find that difficult to bear, too.

I started to browse through the wares on offer. *What a waste*, I thought, *for such a good-looking guy to run a store that had no chance of going viral.*

'Precarity, instability – it usually has a cause,' Kogetsu said. 'Something must be weighing heavily on your mind.'

I almost dropped the little container of *konpeito* I'd picked up. 'How did you know?' I stammered, looking into his golden eyes. His eyelashes were gold, too, and long enough to rest matchsticks on.

'Experience, perhaps,' Kogetsu said with a smirk. 'And intuition. Do those *konpeito* interest you?'

He gestured at the container I had fumbled. It was round and translucent, with a colour gradient from pale purple to blue. The effect reminded me of a hydrangea. But that wasn't what had caught my eye.

'Their name does,' I admitted.

I'd noticed something unusual about the store's wares: all of their names went beyond simple description – MAME DAIFUKU, DORAYAKI, whatever – to include an extra twist.

The container I was holding, for example, was Craving-More Konpeito. After all my worrying about whether I was asking too much of my boyfriend, I'd reached for them almost automatically.

Kogetsu put a finger to his lips, as if about to tell a secret, but what he said next sounded more like something from a fairy tale.

'Eat one of those *konpeito*, and a minor joy will come your way. However, you must not eat more than one per day.'

That explained the name, at least. 'One *konpeito* per day?' I said dubiously. 'That sounds difficult.'

Konpeito were so tiny that it was hard to stop at a handful, let alone one.

'Perhaps so,' Kogetsu said. 'But we take no responsibility for any consequences of over-indulgence.'

I felt my heart skip a beat. His cool expression began to look threatening. What kind of 'conse-quences' were we talking about here?

Kogetsu was such a good actor that for a moment I felt genuine fear. But I didn't want him to know that, so I pushed the container into his hands and said I'd take it. The price tag said it cost just 300 yen, and the individual *konpeito* inside looked big and tasty, so it seemed like a reasonable purchase.

Kogetsu rang up my purchase at an antique cash register and put my *konpeito* in a sepia-coloured paper bag for me. 'Thank you very much,' he said. 'And please be sure to follow the guidelines for usage . . . and dosage.'

*

Safely back home and lying on my bed, I gazed at the *konpeito* on my desk across the bedroom. What a weird experience. But I had to admit, Kogetsu was perceptive. Maybe he had a side hustle as a fortune teller? That would jibe with the mysterious atmosphere of his store, and his dramatic manner.

'I should just try one,' I said aloud, rising from the bed. I'd already had dinner. And I hadn't brushed my teeth yet. So why not?

I shook a few *konpeito* out into my hand – but then remembered Kogetsu's warning and put all but one back.

I wasn't scared. I just wanted to play along with the story.

At least that's what I told myself.

I popped the *konpeito* into my mouth, which immediately filled with the powerful sweetness of pure sugar. There was a hint of peppermint, too, just enough to keep the taste from becoming cloying. It was delicious. And I was supposed to stick to just one per day?

Still . . .

I was too old to believe in jinxes and charms, but if these *konpeito* really could bring me a 'minor joy' of some kind, 300 yen was a bargain.

There was still some time before I had to sleep,

so I decided to prepare for tomorrow's classes. But no sooner had I sat down than my phone trilled from my pillow where I'd left it.

Recognizing the sound as a call instead of a text, I was across the room in one leap. The display showed my boyfriend's name.

I tapped the button to accept the call, and stuttered out, 'H-hello?' I was so nervous that my voice briefly went falsetto. We hadn't talked on the phone in ages.

'Kana?' my boyfriend said. 'Is this a good time?'

'Sure,' I said. 'What's up? You hardly ever call these days.'

'I just finished a big practice exam at my cram school. I can chat for a while today.' He sounded relaxed and cheerful. The practice exam must have gone well.

'Really? That's great!' I said.

'Yeah, I thought I should call you for once, since you're always the one who has to contact me.'

Those words went straight to my heart.

And that wasn't all. He usually did more listening than talking, but today he made an effort to keep the conversation going. He recounted a joke his teacher had told in class, and a silly mistake his friend had made. When I shared my own goofy stories from school, he laughed and reacted with full attention.

It was amazing.

When we ended the call an hour later, I was riding a high. I hugged the phone to my chest and let out a warm, contented sigh. I hadn't felt this happy in ages.

Could that really have been because of the *konpeito*? I glanced at the container and thought back to the sweetness on my tongue earlier.

No. It couldn't be. It was just a coincidence.

But the next day, I made sure to toss one into my mouth before I left for school.

I'd barely got to my desk in registration when a friend from another class appeared in the corridor, beckoning me out again. This was unusual in itself. I'd been in the same class as her last year, but now we mostly kept in touch via text. I left my bag on my desk and went to the door.

'Good morning!' I said. 'You're a long way from registration. What's up?'

'I thought you might like these,' she said,

grinning, and handed me two tickets to a movie I'd heard about. It wasn't in theatres yet, but it was already getting buzz from previews.

'Huh?' I said. 'Why would you give these to me?'

'I bought a whole bunch of advance tickets because I wanted the merch that came with them. But I can't watch the movie *that* many times on my own, so I figured I'd share. Your boyfriend's a fan of this anime, right?'

He was. I'd started watching it, too, in fact, so that we could talk about it together. But had I ever told her that?

'The premiere is this Saturday,' my friend continued. 'You two should go see it together.'

I thanked her, genuinely touched. She insisted it was no problem and went back to her homeroom with a smile and a wave.

I quickly texted my boyfriend asking if he wanted to go. His reply came right away: he didn't have cram school that Saturday, so why didn't we go then?

Yes! A date!

I did a fist-pump right there in the corridor.

I'd been granted my second minor joy. I still

wanted to call it coincidence, but the *konpeito* effect was starting to feel very real.

Eat one of those konpeito, *and a minor joy will come your way.*

I recalled the mysterious atmosphere of the Amberglow Candy Store and Kogetsu's uncanny good looks. Anyone who visited that store would walk out wanting to believe in what he was selling.

Clinging to good-luck charms wasn't my style, but I decided to keep trusting the *konpeito* for as long as these 'minor joys' continued.

From that point on, bad days were a thing of the past. My lucky streak continued: I won a prize in a convenience-store lottery and the classwork I'd happened to be revising came up on a mini-test . . . Nothing life-changing, but more than enough to break up the monotony of high-school life.

My movie date with my boyfriend also went perfectly. He even gave me a present: a mechanical pencil that matched his own, 'so that you won't be lonely while I'm in exam mode.' The design was simple and mature – nothing like my usual pencil, which had a cartoon mascot on it. This unexpected gesture on no particular occasion brought me to tears, which startled my boyfriend. 'I didn't think you'd like it *that* much,' he said.

Then, towards the end of May, the first midterms of the school year rolled around.

As soon as the teachers handed out their study guides, the third-years in the library and study rooms started to look more tightly wound. My phone went completely silent, with no communication from my boyfriend at all. Before I knew it, I was back to worrying if calling him would be a burden or not.

There were still minor joys during the exam period, but they didn't outweigh the stress of midterms or the loneliness of missing my boyfriend. I was already taking my lucky streak for granted.

On the last day of midterms, I caught myself sighing as I wrote in the answers with my new mechanical pencil. Normally, the end of midterms felt like pure freedom, but not this year. I was confident about the exams themselves – I'd done some serious studying to distract myself from my loneliness. But my boyfriend had a practice exam at cram school coming up, too, and he'd still be busy studying for it after my exams were over. He didn't have a choice: classes at his cram school were divided by academic level, and if he did poorly on the test, he'd be transferred to a lower class.

But just because he had no choice didn't mean I was fine with it.

I went home and flopped onto my bed, still feeling antsy and frustrated. Midterms were finally over, but I didn't feel like watching TV or reading manga or any of the things I usually threw myself into eagerly.

I rolled the *konpeito* container around on my palm. After so many days of eating the candy inside, it was now about half-full.

Not everything could be resolved by minor joys. That was a disappointing realization, especially given how invincible I'd felt at first.

However, you must not eat more than one per day.

So far, I'd obeyed Kogetsu's rules to the letter, but what would happen if I broke them? He never did explain what the 'consequences' he'd mentioned were . . .

If eating one *konpeito* per day brought minor joys, would eating a whole handful at once bring a *major* joy?

I still didn't know why this was prohibited, but the desire to give it a try began to well up inside me.

What the heck – go for it!

This encouragement from the devil on my shoulder was all I needed. I opened the container, shook out a little pile of *konpeito* onto the palm of my hand, and brought it to my lips.

The *konpeito* were a mouthful. Their sweetness brought tears to my eyes and it took a while to crunch them all up between my teeth.

The container was now only about a quarter full, but I had no regrets. If anything, I felt a lot better, like the way you do after a good snacking binge.

'Kana!' my mother called from below. 'Dinnertime!'

'Coming!'

When I reached the dining room, I saw a pot of my favourite chicken and tomato stew on the table. Better yet, the side dish was cod roe and potato salad. I loved that salad, but it was so much trouble to make that my mother hardly ever did.

'Yay!' I said, taking my seat at the table 'My favourites!'

My mother chuckled. 'Today was your last day of midterms, wasn't it? You really seemed to buckle down and study this time, so I thought you deserved a reward.'

'Right . . .' I said. 'Thank you.'

I *had* buckled down, but I still felt guilty, because I was hiding the real reason from her. The idea of discussing my boyfriend troubles with her was mortifying.

But this dinner was the *konpeito* already taking effect, right? It was only a minor stroke of luck, but maybe bigger things were on the way.

My father sat down at the table, too, after turning the television on to watch as we ate, as usual. As we were enjoying our dinner, he suddenly frowned at something on the screen. 'Isn't that our city?' he asked.

'Huh?' I looked at the television and saw the familiar name of a cram school.

'They're temporarily closing the school due to bribery suspicions?' my mother said. 'How terrible. Do any of your friends go there, Kana? . . . Kana?'

But I didn't even hear her.

'It can't be,' I said, white as a sheet. The cram

school being investigated for bribery was my boyfriend's.

I no longer had an appetite. Reassuring my worried parents that I was just tired from midterms, I excused myself from the table and retreated into my room.

I fell onto my bed shivering.

Could this also be because of the *konpeito*? Had I put my boyfriend's cram school at risk of closing for good?

I'd often wished he didn't have to go to cram school. I'd see him way more often, and we'd at least be able to walk home together.

'But . . . I didn't mean . . .'

I'd never wanted something like *this* to happen.

My phone trilled. I had a text. I checked it with dread, and as expected it was from my boyfriend. His cram school would be closed for a while, he said; apparently it was already making the news.

The text was short and simple, which wasn't like him at all. Neither was the complete lack of emojis. I could practically feel his low spirits through the screen.

But I couldn't bring myself to call him, so I

texted him back to tell him I'd seen the news and was worried about him.

I was terrified of what tomorrow might bring. Given how many *konpeito* had been in that handful I'd eaten, there was no way this was over yet.

I don't need any more joys, I thought. *Please just let the effects wear off!*

That night I fell asleep trembling.

The next day, since cram school had been cancelled, my boyfriend invited me to walk home with him once classes were over.

When I asked him about it, he seemed nonchalant enough. 'Nothing's been decided yet,' he said. 'If that school shuts down, I'll find a new one.'

But I could tell it was false bravado. He made sure to smile and act like he always did, but when I glanced across at him during lulls in our conversation, his expression was brooding and grave.

At the corner where we went separate ways, he asked if I'd like to study with him that weekend at the library. The idea of spending the weekend with him, too, should have made me happy, but I couldn't muster much enthusiasm for it this time.

How much fun could we have together if he was stressed and I was constantly worried about him?

We take no responsibility for any consequences of overindulgence . . .

Was this my punishment for going too far? Was it a warning not to get too greedy for everything to go my way? To be satisfied with the minor joys instead?

I spent the next day waiting for disaster to strike, but when the end of the school day arrived without incident, I relaxed a little.

I hadn't eaten any *konpeito* the day before, and today had been uneventful. Maybe the effects really had worn off. I sneaked a peek at the container hidden in my schoolbag – I was too worried about what might happen if I left it at home – and breathed a sigh of relief.

Our midterm grades had come back today. Mine were better than expected, as was my rank in class. I'd even climbed into the average range for maths, my worst subject. I was happy not to be lower, but a little disappointed that this was the best I could do after all that studying. Evidently, I'd need to do more than cram right before the test if I wanted better grades. Academically oriented schools were tough.

But my boyfriend had been studying ever since starting his third year. He must have got great grades.

When we met at the school gates, though, there was a dark shadow over his face.

'Did you get your midterm grades?' he asked, before I could ask him.

'Um . . . yeah,' I said. We were still right outside the school, and I was uncomfortably aware of all the other students around. 'My class rank improved a little. How about you?'

'My grades were better than last time, but my overall rank dropped,' he said.

It wasn't the reply I'd expected. I was lost for words for a moment.

'But . . . you studied so hard,' I said at last. He'd been revising and drilling the material all year, not just before the test like me.

'I wasn't the only one who got serious about studying this year,' he said. 'Especially the kids in school clubs – once they step back from club activities in third year, their grades go way up. I thought going to that cram school would keep me ahead, but I guess I was going too easy on myself.'

I heard self-mockery in his voice. It was true that his class felt much more intense this year, and I knew a lot of his classmates had got serious about academics, too. But I hadn't expected things to get this tough for him.

'If I can't turn this around, I might need to rethink which schools I apply to,' he said. 'My parents told me that public college is all we can afford. If I don't get a spot at one of those, I might not be able to go at all.'

'Don't say that!' I blurted out. He'd told me before that his family wasn't that well off, so he wouldn't be able to apply to private colleges. But I'd blithely assumed that since he was a good student (unlike me), he'd be fine.

'Sorry,' my boyfriend said. 'I'm overthinking it, I know. I really trusted my cram-school teacher, so maybe that scandal is hitting me harder than I thought.'

His tone was cheerful, but his smile didn't reach his eyes. I realized for the first time that he had bags under them, and it didn't look like he'd brushed his hair that morning.

I was always so proud of the attention my boy-friend paid to his appearance. Had I been seeing him as some sort of perfect being? Someone who could be strong in any situation, never raising his voice in protest?

He wasn't, of course. He was a year older, but he was still a high-school student, just like me. The fact he was struggling with the news about his cram school and his best efforts not working out made complete sense.

'Kana?' he said, his eyes widening. 'What's wrong?'

Tears were trickling down my cheeks. 'I . . . I think this is my fault,' I said. I hugged myself with shivering arms, feeling goosebumps rise on my skin.

'Kana . . . ?'

'Your cram school closing might be all my fault!'

By then I was sobbing. He took my hand and led me to a quieter side street with fewer people around.

'What do you mean, all your fault?' he asked, putting a gentle hand on my shoulder. 'It's okay. Take a deep breath and tell me about it.'

Sobs subsiding to hiccups, I told him about buying the mysterious *konpeito*, the minor joys I'd enjoyed since, and even my luck with the movie ticket.

'But it wasn't enough for me,' I said. 'Kogetsu told me to only eat one a day, but I broke my promise and ate a whole handful at once!'

If only I could turn back time to that day! I'd slap those *konpeito* out of my own hand if I had to.

'It's my fault for getting greedy!' I said. 'I wanted to spend more time with you because it makes me happy, but I didn't even think about how it would affect you. I didn't realize until now how pointless happiness is if the people around you are miserable. I'm sorry!'

After I got all this out in a rush, I sank into a squat, hugging my schoolbag. I felt completely drained, unable even to stand up.

'Kana . . .'

I'd expected my boyfriend to be disappointed or make fun of me for believing what Kogetsu had told me, but instead he wore a serious, thoughtful look.

'Do you have those *konpeito* with you right now?'

'Y-Yes,' I said. 'I was afraid to leave them at home, so . . . they're in my bag.'

I unzipped my schoolbag, dug out the *konpeito* container, and handed it to him. He examined it curiously. There were so few *konpeito* left that you could see the bottom.

I'd resigned myself to him laughing off the whole fantastical story, so I was surprised by his careful attention. Did he actually believe me?

'These look like normal *konpeito* to me,' he said. 'I guess they're not mass-market, though – the container doesn't have a label, and this decorative cord is pretty distinctive.'

He opened the lid and sniffed the contents.

'Smells like peppermint,' he muttered, then said to me, 'One a day, you said?'

I realized what he was about to do. 'Wait!' I cried.

But before I could stop him, he'd popped a *konpeito* into his mouth.

'Spit it out, quickly!' I urged, scrambling to my feet and snatching back the container. 'You don't know what might happen!'

'Sure I do,' my boyfriend said. 'I'm obeying the one-per-day rule, so only good things will happen, right?'

'Well, that is the rule . . . but still . . .'

As I anxiously watched him chew the *konpeito*, I heard a phone ring.

'Sorry, that's me,' my boyfriend said. He pulled his phone from his pocket and checked the screen. 'Huh. My cram school.' He glanced at me. I nodded, and he answered the phone.

'Hello? . . . That's right . . . Yes. Wait, really?!'

I couldn't hear the voice at the other end, but I could hear my boyfriend's rise as his face filled with surprise.

When he ended the call, he looked at me with a radiant smile. The dark clouds from before were completely gone.

'Great news!' he said. 'Those bribery suspicions came to nothing. The cram school's reopening again!'

'Really?! I'm so glad!'

I hadn't dreamed that the news would have to retract its story so quickly. My boyfriend's cheeks were flushed with excitement.

'If I can keep taking classes there, I think I can do better at finals,' he said. 'I'll have to try extra hard the next time cram school holds its ranking exams!'

'Yes,' I said. 'I'm really glad everything cleared up so quickly.'

Was this happening because my boyfriend had eaten that *konpeito*?

Of course, I thought. *Why didn't I see it earlier?*

If I'd wanted to improve our relationship, I should have shared the *konpeito* with him right from the start. It was obvious, but in my self-absorption it hadn't even occurred to me.

'That takes care of that, then,' my boyfriend said. 'Nothing more for you to worry about – right?'

He held a hand out to me where I stood, frozen to the spot.

But I didn't take it. I only shook my head.

'No,' I said. 'This whole scare has made me realize something. I don't have the right to be your girlfriend.'

He stared at me, his mouth open with shock. Then his face twisted into a grimace. 'So . . . you're fed up with me?'

'No!' I shouted. 'I'm fed up with *myself*!'

I clenched my fists, hot tears welling under my eyelids again.

'I really like you,' I said. 'But now that I know

how selfish I can be, I'm worried that I might get greedy and make trouble for you again.'

My boyfriend stared at me, holding my gaze. I braced for him to say *Fine, then. Let's break up.*

But instead, he shook his head.

'If you're selfish, then so am I,' he said. 'When you asked me to be your boyfriend, I said yes, even though I knew I'd have to concentrate on studying this year. I wanted to get good grades *and* enjoy life as a high-school couple.'

'R-really . . . ?' I said. 'I thought you saying yes was just a lucky break for me.'

'Are you kidding? I've known you since junior high, and I've always liked you and thought you were cute. *That's* the reason I said yes.'

I felt my cheeks go hot and looked down. I hadn't known he felt that way.

'I had no idea that you were feeling so lonely because of me studying all the time,' my boyfriend said. 'I'm just as greedy and selfish as you.'

'I didn't realize any of this,' I said. 'You always seem so cool and collected – ready to deal with whatever might happen.'

'Because I'm desperately trying to impress you,'

he said. 'To be honest, right now my heart's pounding with terror that telling you all this will make you stop liking me.'

He gave me a wry smile, and I finally saw that he was just like the guys in my own class – a regular, everyday boy.

'No chance of that!' I said. 'If anything, I like you more than ever.'

'Thanks,' he said, patting my head. 'Anyway, from now on, let's talk our problems out with each other, just like we did today. No *konpeito* necessary.'

'Okay,' I said, fighting back more tears. 'Thank you.'

As I struggled to keep my sobs in, my boyfriend pulled me in for a hug. He was tall enough for my face to be completely buried in his chest. I wrapped my arms around him and felt my heart beat faster.

We stood like that in silence for a while, and when we let go of each other, we were both wearing bashful expressions.

'From now on, I'll talk to you about my worries, instead of keeping them to myself,' I said.

'I'd like that,' he said.

I'd been so determined to play the understanding

girlfriend, to not seem needy, that I'd resigned myself to suffer in silence.

That was the mistake that had started it all. There were plenty of problems one person couldn't solve, but everything felt more manageable when you had someone else to help.

Instead of eating the remaining *konpeito* myself, I shared them with family and friends. 'Eat this, and a minor joy will come your way,' I'd tell them, and their eyes would shine with excitement, as if they were drawing fortunes at a shrine.

This was how the *konpeito* were meant to be eaten. And imagining the good things that might happen with others was a minor joy in itself.

'Are you sure you should be giving away good luck like this?' one of my classmates had asked, looking dubiously at the *konpeito* I'd given her.

'Definitely,' I said. 'I want everyone to enjoy it!'

Because I'd finally realized: seeing the people I cared about happy made me happy, too.

One day after school, I made my way back to the shrine, but the path at the rear of the precinct had vanished. Even the gap in the trees was gone.

Had the shopping street I'd visited that day been real? Did the Amberglow Candy Store truly exist? I was starting to wonder.

'Maybe a fox was playing tricks on me?' I muttered to myself. But then I imagined Kogetsu scowling *I would never*, and I let out a giggle.

*

On the roof of the main shrine building, looking down at the girl below, stood a figure illuminated by the evening sun. The figure was wearing a kimono and *hakama* and had fox ears and a tail.

'The truth is, eating a handful of *konpeito* at once has no particular effect,' Kogetsu mused. 'The minor joy arrives as usual, but that is all. Perhaps my warning was too ominous.'

He sounded more tickled than remorseful.

'I see now that guilt can lead humans to see patterns in sheer coincidence, connecting it to their own actions. An unexpected finding.'

Kogetsu narrowed his eyes in a smile as his tail swished.

'Now, then – time to complete the usual exchange.'

Kogetsu raised one hand. The *konpeito* container emerged from the schoolbag on the girl's back and returned to his hand, glowing as it floated through the air.

'When humans realize they are being greedy, then, this is how they react. Most intriguing.'

Kogetsu took the single remaining *konpeito* from the container and blew on it. In a moment, the pale violet candy was encased in amber.

'Another sample of emotion acquired. But my collection is not complete yet.'

The girl below then felt around in her schoolbag for the vanished container, tilting her head curiously. The corners of Kogetsu's mouth twitched in the faintest hint of a smile. A moment later, he was gone.

CHAPTER 2

Invisible Wasanbon

'Welcome to _____ _____ Property. My name is Ayumu Koguma, and I'll be assisting you today.'

When I presented my business card along with this self-introduction, the young newlyweds across the table from me both struggled to keep a straight face.

Koguma, my surname, literally means 'little bear'. *Ayumu* means 'walk'. The combination invariably made people imagine a little bear cub toddling towards them.

'Th-that's a cute name,' the wife said, trying to smooth over their suppressed laughter. But her husband's cheeks were still twitching.

I chuckled. 'I get that a lot,' I said. 'It's not a common surname, I know.'

But I knew that it wasn't the rarity or even the cuteness of my name that made them laugh.

When I was first assigned to this branch, the manager had clapped me on the shoulder and said, 'Do you realize how lucky you are to have that name with your looks, Koguma? Talk about a conversation-starter! Take my word for it – you're cut out for customer service!'

He was right on one count. My name was one thing, but it was my looks that really got a reaction.

I was short and plump, with a little pot belly. My face was round, and my features were small and mild, without any hint of aggression in them. I looked like a cartoon bear who lives to eat honey.

If I'd been able to embrace it, to joke about it myself and win people over, that would have been fine. But to do that, I would have needed quick wits and solid communication skills. And, frankly, I had neither.

I'd been a cheerful boy, unconcerned with my looks. I only became self-conscious and desperate to avoid attracting notice in junior high school, after a certain incident changed everything.

It happened after school. I'd left the classroom already, but had come back to get something I'd forgotten. As I arrived at the door, I realized that a few of my female classmates were still inside chatting about boys. One of them was the girl I had a secret crush on. I knew it was wrong to eavesdrop, but I couldn't resist. I stayed out of sight behind the door and listened.

The topic of conversation was which of the boys in class they would consider dating. Eventually, my name came up.

'What about Koguma?'

'That goofy little guy? No way! He's more like a mascot than a man!'

The girl who'd laughed off the suggestion was the one I had a crush on.

More like a mascot than a man. When I heard this assessment, I realized for the first time that my appearance was so distinctive that it prompted people to make jokes about it.

My adolescent pride was left in tatters. From that day on, what should have been the best years of my life were dull and grey instead. I did my best to be quiet and inoffensive, so that no one would laugh at or bully me. I mastered the art of fading into the background and faking smiles.

I also tried losing weight, of course. But with my

round face and roly-poly frame, dropping pounds didn't make me look slim or sleek – just shrivelled. My friends worried about me, saying I looked like a haggard, insubstantial shadow of my former self. So I decided to be a chubby, healthy-looking shrimp instead of a shrivelled, gaunt one.

I lived my life as quietly as possible – but things changed when I entered the workforce. I got a job with an estate agency, which, bafflingly enough, assigned me to customer service. My colleagues at the counter were beautiful and well-groomed. And all I could think was, *What am I doing here?*

Whenever I introduced myself to a customer, I got a snort of laughter in response. Feeling like my name and appearance were constantly being mocked made every day dreary.

*

'Ugh . . .'

I was trudging wearily back to the office after a long day of visiting properties. It was late in the afternoon, but the rainy season had just ended and it was still brutally hot and humid. I would start to sweat through my shirt as soon as I stepped outside.

'I really don't think I'm cut out for this kind of work,' I sighed.

Earlier today, a tough-looking customer with bleached hair had kept telling me to speak up. And when I'd gone to inspect some properties with a female client, the sweat had poured off me throughout my sales pitch. When I'd used my handkerchief to wipe my face, she'd laughed at me.

I was a heavy perspirer by nature, but it was always compounded by my nerves around being alone with a woman. It had begun on that traumatic day in junior high, but it was now so deep-rooted that I even got anxious when I noticed a female colleague glancing my way across the room as she spoke to someone else. I would find myself wondering darkly if she was secretly badmouthing me to them.

Lately I'd been thinking of changing jobs. My prospects of finding something better seemed slim, but my boss refused to even consider moving me to a different department. I'd joined the company as a new graduate three years ago, and now I was twenty-five. It seemed like just the right age to think about a career change.

My boss, the branch manager, encouraged me like a school sports coach might. 'I'm telling you, customer service is where you shine,' he'd say. 'Make those pitches with confidence.'

But I *had* no confidence in myself, which is why I couldn't use the high-pressure techniques my younger, more handsome colleagues did. I couldn't bring myself to say *This is definitely the better choice* and point at the property with the higher rent, or boldly offer unsolicited opinions like *If it were me, I'd go for this one*.

Sometimes a customer would ask my opinion when they were struggling to decide between multiple options, but even then I'd fret and vacillate: *Well, I'd go for this one – oh, but the other one does have some tempting advantages – hmm* . . . Ultimately, I wouldn't be able to choose at all.

'I wish I were invisible. Then I could reach my full potential without worrying about how I looked.'

Was it such an unreasonable wish? It wasn't like I was asking to be head-turningly hot.

Speaking of which, the lingering summer heat

was killing me. I'd already finished the bottle of water I'd brought with me, and I didn't see any cafés or drink vending machines in the area. I still had quite a way to go before I reached the office, and if I couldn't rest and cool down, I at least wanted to replenish my fluids a little.

Just as I was starting to wheeze from overheating, a run-down old shrine caught my eye.

'Huh?'

I'd never noticed it before, despite visiting this area many times.

Why not offer a prayer, ask for help from the kami, and see if there were any vending machines on the shrine precinct? I started climbing the stone staircase to the shrine.

I passed through the torii gate and entered the shrine precinct proper. The densely flourishing trees that surrounded the precinct cast a lot of shade, making it the perfect place to cool down. No vending machine, though, I surmised, looking around. It wasn't surprising. The shrine was so tiny it didn't even have an office.

I dropped some change into the coin box, bowed my head, and put my hands together.

I want to be invisible. And if I can't be invisible, I at least want my boss to consider moving me to a different department. A negative sort of prayer, but there you have it.

I bowed once more and turned away from the shrine. It was in that moment that I sensed something was off, and turned to look back again.

There it was. At the very back of the precinct, behind the shrine itself, I noticed a gap in the surrounding trees.

I approached cautiously, wondering why this might be. But what I saw was nothing like what I expected.

The gap led to a road that stretched away from the shrine, and at the end of the road was a weathered old shopping street. It seemed a fairly new residential area, but the shopping street was decidedly retro, as if someone had cut out a slice of time and preserved it carefully.

A smell like incense wafted from the gap in the foliage, and I shivered, feeling goosebumps rise on my arms.

It wasn't a good sign to feel a cold chill when it was this hot. I needed fluids, and fast, or I was at risk of heatstroke. I was sure my boss wouldn't mind a slight detour on my way back to the office, under the circumstances.

Still thinking of excuses, I walked into the street.

The unsurfaced road felt like hardened sand, and seemed to catch at my leather shoes, which were more accustomed to asphalt. On both sides of the street, most of the stores had taken their signs down for the day, with nothing visible through the dark windows.

No doubt it was one of those 'shuttered streets' you heard about, left behind and forgotten as the residential area modernized around it and its people found other places to shop. But some people preferred the older community feel, so revitalizing this shopping street could give the neighbourhood broader appeal.

I realized I was looking at it through my work glasses again. I struggled with customer service, but I did like working in residential property.

Some things about the street still confused me, though. What was with the red and white lanterns, and the signs written in characters I couldn't read? The atmosphere was unique, seeming to combine Japanese and Chinese elements.

I noticed a streetside banner that read
LEMONADE – REFRESHING SWEETS. Behind
it was a hole in the wall with a counter at it, like
a cigarette stand. I guessed it was the old-school
equivalent of a juice bar.

'Um – excuse me!' I called into the darkness
beyond the counter. 'I'd like to buy a bottle of
lemonade?'

After a moment, a hand emerged from the
gloom and placed a bright blue lemonade bottle
on the counter.

'Eep!' I said, startled. 'That was a surprise.'

A *here you are* would have been nice. Evidently
the proprietor was as customer-service-averse as I
was. That, or they had a serious lack of motivation.

'Thank you,' I said. 'I'll, uh . . . leave the money
here.'

I put a hundred-yen coin on the counter and
hurried away.

I'd been given an old-school lemonade bottle,
sealed with a marble instead of a cap. I thumbed the
marble in and chugged the whole bottle. It was cool
and sweet and I felt a lot better afterwards.

My heatstroke was now averted, but I decided

to check out the rest of the street before leaving. It couldn't hurt to know what was here.

When I reached the T-junction at the far end, I saw a store with a pink lantern outside. The sun was just setting, and the store seemed to melt into the orange light in a captivating way. The sign outside read Amberglow Candy Store.

The building looked old, but it was in gleaming good repair – nothing like the dusty stores surrounding it. The engraved wooden door and the pink lantern outside were Chinese in style, but the overall design was Japanese, giving it an international feel. The cryptic name and peculiar opening hours – it claimed to be 'closed on the new and full moon' – added to the mystery.

As a fan of buildings with unusual exteriors, I felt a strong urge welling within me to go inside. In my experience, stores like this were usually run by highly idiosyncratic and demanding people. As I pushed open the front door, I imagined the proprietor I might find inside. Beard, round glasses, a vaguely hippie-ish demeanour . . . ? But then –

'Welcome.'

'Wah!'

The cool voice came from so close to the door that I yelped and leapt into the air.

'I apologize,' the voice said. 'Did I startle you?'

The voice belonged to a young man so handsome I blinked involuntarily at the sight of him. He had silky golden hair and wore dark *hakama* trousers, and the look worked surprisingly well for him.

'I sensed a human customer, so I thought I might offer a proper welcome. Clearly my approach has room for improvement.'

'Uh . . . yeah,' I said. A somewhat flat response to his theatrical pronouncements.

He didn't look like I'd imagined, but he was clearly the idiosyncratic, opinionated type.

'I am Kogetsu, the proprietor of the store,' he said. 'Please take all the time you wish to browse.' Then he made a small bow and stationed himself behind the counter at the store's rear.

Apparently, if you were attractive enough, you could make a living running a store even in a half-deserted shopping street like this. He probably didn't have a care in the world. I felt a flash of envy.

My breathing was back to normal, so I looked around the store's interior properly. Its wares were laid out on waist-high tables lit by dim lanternlight. Some were traditional *wagashi* made using the sweet bean paste called *anko* – there was *nerikiri*, for example, and *yokan* – but there were also retro sweets like candies on strings and boxes of caramels. There was no obvious order to the arrangement, but for some reason there was a strange harmony to it. Maybe it was the signs placed in front of the products.

Each sign bore a product name handwritten with a brush on washi paper, and each name had a slight twist to it. CRAVING-MORE KONPEITO, for example. Why not just call them *konpeito*? Was this part of Kogetsu's vision for the store? What exactly was this 'craving' business?

I strolled around the store, fascinated. Finally, I stopped in front of some boxes of *wasanbon*. The little flowers and animals made of pressed sugar were simple enough. But the sign read INVISIBLE WASANBON.

I remembered wishing I were invisible earlier, and had the unsettling feeling of being seen through entirely.

'Excuse me,' I called to Kogetsu, who was still

behind the counter. 'Why are these *wasanbon* "invisible"?'

'I am sure you are familiar with the way *wasanbon* swiftly dissolve in the mouth,' he said. 'Have you ever wished you could disappear in the same way?'

His narrowed golden eyes seemed to pierce my soul.

After a moment's hesitation, I said, 'I'll take a box.' I still found the situation a little unsettling, but my desire to try the *wasanbon* won out.

'Thank you very much. That will be five hundred yen.'

Even for such a small box, that was cheap for *wasanbon*. I'd probably finish a single box in less than a day, so I decided to buy two instead.

'Here you are, sir,' said Kogetsu, handing me a sepia-coloured paper bag with the *wasanbon* inside. 'Please be sure to observe the usage and dosage guidelines.'

I thrust my purchase into my bag and hurried away from the shopping street.

*

Once the heat of the moment had passed, I kicked myself for buying two boxes of *wasanbon*. Why didn't I at least get two different kinds of candy?

The problem, as I realized when I tried one of the *wasanbon* the following morning, was that they didn't really taste like anything but sugar. They weren't the kind of snack you could binge on.

Still, they seemed pretty shelf-stable. *Guess I'll just eat one every day*, I thought as I left for work.

On the way, I stopped at my usual convenience store to pick up a drink and some lunch for later. When I reached the counter with my coffee, energy drink and *yakiniku* bento, it was unattended. After a few moments passed, it was clear no one was coming either.

But there was an employee stacking shelves right nearby. 'Um . . . Excuse me?' I said.

He turned to look at me, and his eyes went wide. 'Whoa!' he said. 'I'm so sorry, sir – I didn't notice you there! Let me ring you up right away.'

Bowing apologetically, he hurried behind the counter. Based on his appearance, it seemed he was still a student.

I didn't pay it much mind. These things happened.

But as I left the store I heard an older employee, presumably the manager, scolding him.

'He was standing right in front of you! Why didn't you notice?'

'I don't know, sir! I was keeping an eye on the register, but for some reason I didn't see him.'

'Didn't *see* him?! How is that possible?'

I sneaked a parting backward glance through the automatic doors. The younger employee was tilting his head, looking baffled.

The strangeness continued at work.

I watched my boss say, 'Huh? Where'd Koguma go?' and start looking around for me – even though we were in the same room. I presented my card to customers and got no response whatsoever. And when I asked a junior employee in the break room how their day was going, they almost jumped out of their skin. 'Mr Koguma! Where did you come from?!' they asked.

But I'd been in the room when they walked into it.

Hard as it was to believe at first, after that many incidents in one day, I couldn't deny it any longer. I was invisible.

Maybe not technically *invisible*. People could see me, after all. But until I was brought to their attention, I might as well have been the invisible man. And it had to be because of those Invisible Wasanbon from the Amberglow Candy Store.

Maybe Kogetsu was actually the kami of the shrine I'd visited, granting my timid little wish out of pity. That would explain why the store was so strange and why Kogetsu himself, with his golden hair and striking good looks, had seemed vaguely untethered from reality.

No matter how hard I tried in my life, it was always my looks that got all the attention. I couldn't believe I didn't have to worry about that anymore. It was a dream come true.

I got in the habit of popping one of the *wasanbon* into my mouth every morning as I left for work. And I felt like patting myself on the back for buying two boxes. Even eating one piece of *wasanbon* a day, my supply would last me two months. When I ran out, I could just visit that shrine again.

Now that customers weren't reacting to my name or my looks, dealing with them went a lot more smoothly. I was even able to be a little more assertive in my sales pitches, notwithstanding my former struggles. I had no idea how easy it could be. If you knew that no one would laugh at you, no matter what you said, self-confidence came naturally.

My life went from gloomy to glorious, and I arrived at work each day with a spring in my step. A few days later, though, I was unexpectedly reunited with my past.

It started when a young man and woman sat down across from me. I introduced myself as usual, handing over my card. But the moment the woman saw the name on it, she looked up in surprise.

'Wait,' she said, studying my face. 'Is that you, Koguma?'

I hesitated. 'Takada . . . ?'

'That's me!' she said with a delighted, uninhibited laugh. 'Wow! I didn't expect to run into you here! So, you're in property now?'

It was my former crush – the one who'd traumatized me in junior high with her 'He's more like a mascot than a man' comment.

I was hoping she wouldn't notice who I was, but

I couldn't exactly make my name invisible, too. She was ten years older now, but her light brown hair tied back in a ponytail and sporty outfit were completely in line with her image back in school.

'That's right!' I said. 'I understand you're looking for an apartment today?'

'Yep!' she beamed. 'We're getting married. Oh – this is my fiancé, of course . . .'

The man sitting next to Takada bowed his head politely. Takada looked bashful.

'Well!' I said, hiding my shock. 'Congratulations!' I'd thought the man with her was a brother or some other relative.

I mean, just look at him – short and chubby, with a kind-looking face and glasses. He was exactly the same type of guy as me.

And Takada was marrying this man? After what she'd said in junior high? There had to be some kind of mistake.

But as I watched, the two began poring over apartment floor plans together, exchanging opinions and smiles. They were the picture of a happily engaged couple eager to begin married life.

I refused to believe some comforting explanation

about her taste in men changing as she matured. No – he had to be such a great guy that it made up for his looks and then some.

'You know, Koguma, you've changed,' Takada said. 'Until I saw your card, I didn't even realize it was you.'

'Do you think so?' I asked.

'Yeah. How can I put it? You still *look* the same, but you seem less . . . *noticeable*, somehow. Um – sorry. I mean . . .'

Evidently, she still had no filter. Of course, this free-spirited nature was part of what I'd found attractive about her in junior high.

The three of us went out to look at apartments that very day. I drove us around in one of the company cars as we inspected a series of small, tidy places suitable for a couple of newlyweds.

Takada's fiancé had apparently taken a few hours off work for this, but not the whole day. Eventually he politely said that he would leave the rest of the inspections to Takada and me, as he had to return to work. I offered to drive him there, but he demurred, saying it was close enough to walk.

'There are still a few places left on my list of

candidates,' I said to Takada, flipping through my binder of listings. 'Are you sure you don't want to come back when he's free?'

It was just the two of us now, but I wasn't a bit nervous.

'I'm sure,' she said. 'He told me that if I find a place I like, I should sign the lease.'

'Great,' I said. 'He sounds very kind.'

Wives often took the lead in deciding where to live, but Takada's fiancé must really respect her opinion if he didn't even need to see the place before moving in.

At the next apartment, I was walking Takada through the property rattling off selling points when she hesitantly said, 'Listen . . . About junior high . . . ?'

My heart thumped painfully as the scene flashed before my eyes again. There she was, sitting on her desk in her sailor-collared uniform, swinging her legs and laughing at me.

'You heard me that time after school, didn't you?' she said. 'Saying all that mean stuff.'

Just as I'd suspected. *Please, no*, I begged internally. *Don't open the wound any wider*. But she didn't stop talking.

59

'The thing is, I actually –'

'It's fine!' I interrupted. 'It's fine. It doesn't bother me anymore. To be honest, I'm more embarrassed to learn that you knew I was eavesdropping!'

I made a show of scratching my head ruefully. I knew from experience that intercepting these conversations by turning them into jokes made things easier.

'Right,' Takada said slowly. 'Well – anyway, I'm sorry.'

She seemed to have more to say, but I kept my smile fixed and the conversation focused on apartment-hunting, leaving no room to rehash any old embarrassments.

'Thanks for today, Koguma. I'm really happy with the place you helped me find.'

Takada had been taken by the last property we inspected, and signed a provisional lease on the spot.

I never had let her finish what she'd been trying to say, but her apology had gone some way towards softening the trauma I'd carried since junior high. Most importantly, learning that she'd realized I was eavesdropping and felt guilty about it ever since almost overwrote the original unpleasant memory.

But none of that felt like a reason to throw away my recently obtained panacea. Things were so much easier for me now. I didn't have to worry about what people thought of me if they didn't see me at all.

I'd always compensated for my chubbiness by taking extra care with my grooming, ensuring there were no unruly cowlicks or missed patches of stubble that might have bothered my customers. In the summer, I used deodorant and kept a spare vest and shirt in my locker. I even tried to tread lightly as I walked around, and made myself as small as possible when I passed someone. And I made sure never to do something like casually pat a female colleague on the back, because I was sure they would find any physical contact with me unpleasant.

All that was behind me now. I no longer needed to anxiously monitor the faces around me for disapproval. What a wonderful way to live!

And that was why I kept eating one piece of *wasanbon* every day.

*

'We've always been the top branch in our area, but this month our lease numbers have dropped – and they've taken our overall earnings down with them,' the branch manager shared at our regular end-of-month meeting.

I wasn't especially bothered by the troubling news, since I didn't see any connection to my performance.

My own sales figures were as high as ever, and becoming more confident in my dealings with customers meant that my lease numbers from walk-ins were up as well.

It didn't seem that any particular employee had dropped off, in fact. I assumed it was just one of those unlucky months.

Which is why, when the branch manager asked to see me privately afterwards, I was expecting a cheerful pat on the back.

But in that case, why was his face so grim?

'Take a seat, Koguma,' he said.

'Y-yes, sir . . .'

I sat opposite him at the long desk in the break room. He folded his hands under his chin, saying nothing at first. The silence in the room started to feel oppressive.

Finally, he ran a hand through his slicked-back hair and heaved a deep sigh.

I might have stopped worrying about what other people thought, but this gesture still made me shrink reflexively. My meekness was too ingrained to disappear in less than a month.

'I gather your approach to customer service has changed lately?' he asked.

This was exactly the question I'd been expecting. I exhaled with relief.

'Yes, sir,' I said. 'I've found my self-confidence, just like you told me to, and that makes it easier to be assertive with –'

I crisply launched into the speech I'd prepared, but he shook his head before I was finished.

'You've got it all wrong, Koguma,' he said. 'I did tell you to have more confidence, but this isn't what I meant.'

'It isn't . . . ?'

I was so shocked I wasn't sure how to reply.

'It's my fault for not being clearer,' he said, 'but I didn't want you to start acting like this.'

'Wh-what do you mean?' I stammered.

'Get comfortable,' he said. 'This might take a

while.' And then, calmly and quietly, he began to explain some things that I found truly unbelievable.

He told me that my low-pressure customer service had been popular with women and our more retiring customers. That he'd known this, and made a point of steering those customers my way.

And that my recent shift in gear had made our branch less able to get these customers to sign leases, which was why our figures had dropped.

'When we had a customer the others couldn't handle, I sent them to you. You picked up the business we would have lost otherwise – that's why our figures were good in the first place. And the reason you could do that was your empathetic, customer-centric approach to sales.'

He looked me straight in the eye as he said this, making sure I got the message.

'I had no idea,' I said, my voice trembling as I struggled to put all the pieces together.

But now that he'd mentioned it, I realized I very rarely found myself dealing with our more aggressive and outgoing customers. They were always handled by a good-looking junior employee.

My boss had been assigning me the work I was best suited to all along.

'I'm glad you feel more confident talking to customers now,' he said, fixing me with a penetrating gaze. 'But are you sure you haven't forgotten something important along the way?'

I thought back on my former approach to sales.

I would carefully watch my customers' faces as I did my best to explain everything. My mind would constantly be racing, trying to identify the things they were still unclear on and the additional information they might need to make a decision. And when I sensed that a customer wanted time to think things over, I would sit back and let them have it, without saying a word.

I couldn't have done any of this without observing them closely. Without even realizing it, I'd been practicing an empathetic, customer-centric approach to sales, just like my boss said.

But what about recently? Had becoming invisible made me more complacent about all that? At the very least, I had to admit that I wasn't giving much thought to my customers' feelings of late. As long as they signed on the dotted line of a property

I recommended, regardless of what had brought them to that point, I was satisfied.

'I know you worry about your appearance,' my boss said. 'But I'm telling you, Koguma, looking harmless and kind is an asset in our line of work. That's what I wanted you to have confidence in. I definitely didn't mean you should throw away your good qualities.'

Of course. Hadn't my boss always said I was cut out for sales, right from the start? I was the one who hadn't taken him seriously. In my bitterness, I'd stubbornly focused solely on the negative side of things.

'I've certainly never thought the way you looked was a negative. I don't think anyone has. To be honest, the female employees often tell me I could learn a bit about kindness from you,' he added with a rueful smile on his grizzled face.

For all my fretting about my appearance, no one had cared about it anywhere near as much as I had.

As I followed my boss out of the break room, I heard someone call, 'Koguma!'

I turned to see Kazama, one of the female employees. She was twenty-four, a year younger than me, and her unfailingly cheerful smile helped keep the whole branch's morale high.

I wasn't sure what she was doing in the corridor in that moment. It was almost as if she'd been waiting for someone, but I was probably overthinking it.

'Hi, Kazama,' I said. 'Did you need something?'

Kazama watched our boss walk down the corridor and into a different room, then said in a low voice, 'I heard the boss pulled you in for a meeting. Is everything all right?'

'Oh, sure,' I said. 'I got a bit of a lecture, but I have to admit it took a lot of weight off my shoulders.'

'Weight off your shoulders?'

Kazama tilted her head curiously, but when she saw I wasn't going to elaborate, she didn't press any further. Instead, she started anxiously wringing her hands. What had got into her today?

'So,' I said awkwardly. 'You just wanted to make sure I was okay?'

'Yes – I mean – well, actually, no. Th-there was one other thing.' She didn't quite meet my eyes as she stuttered, but she did keep stealing glances at me. I was never good at reading people at times like this, and I felt guilty about that now.

Finally, Kazama seemed to find her resolve. 'Listen,' she said. 'Would you like to go out for drinks tonight? Just the two of us. I want to get your opinion on something.'

'*My* opinion? Are you sure?'

I couldn't hide my astonishment. It was the first time in my life a woman had asked me out socially. And I often noticed Kazama glancing my way from across the office as she talked with other colleagues; I'd always assumed she was complaining about me.

But she just nodded, still wringing her hands. 'You're the one I want to talk to,' she said.

What could she possibly want my opinion on? It was probably safe to rule out boyfriend troubles, at least. On the other hand, if she was thinking of quitting or switching jobs, I wasn't sure I'd be able to persuade her to stay.

But the look in her eyes made it clear she was counting on me, so I didn't want to turn her down.

'O-okay,' I said. 'Sure. I'll think of a good place for a chat.'

'Thank you!'

Discussing our options later, we realized that neither of us actually drank alcohol, so instead of going to an izakaya we decided to get dinner at an Italian place.

At the restaurant, once we'd finished our antipasti and the main course had arrived, the mood felt relaxed enough to try opening up.

'I'm still in shock,' I said. 'This is the first time a woman's ever invited me out to eat.'

Kazama stared at me in shock, a forkful of Genovese pasta halfway to her mouth. 'Really?' she said, eyes wide. 'But you're so gentle and kind. I thought you'd get all kinds of attention from women.'

'Try none!' I said. 'Back in junior high, someone once said I might make a cute enough mascot, but they couldn't see me as a man.'

By now I was able to joke about my trauma, but Kazama only frowned thoughtfully.

'Was it a girl who said that?' she asked.

'Yes, one of my classmates.'

'Are you sure she wasn't just trying to hide her embarrassment? Maybe she actually had a crush on you.'

I was so surprised I dropped my fork. It hit my

plate with a hard metallic sound that reverberated between us.

'No way!' I said. 'It really wasn't like that.'

I was breaking out in a cold sweat, so I drained my water glass with one big gulp. In my consternation, though, it went down the wrong pipe.

'Are you all right?' Kazama asked with concern as I coughed.

I knew I was falling pitifully short of suave charm. But this was who I was. Instead of trying to pretend I was something more, why not embrace the good qualities I did have?

'The truth is, I thought you didn't like me either,' I said to Kazama. 'So I'm glad you invited me out.'

'Me?' Kazama said, eyes wide, her finger pointed at her nose. Then, hesitantly, she asked, 'Is this . . . because you noticed me talking to other women in the office about you?'

'Yeah,' I said. 'You seemed to glance my way a lot while you talked, so I figured you were making fun of me.'

'Oh, *no-o-o*,' Kazama said, clutching her head in her hands. 'Of course you'd get the wrong idea. I'm so sorry. But I wasn't complaining about you to them. I was saying things like, "Have you seen Koguma today? He looks so cute, just like a bear," and "Guess what? I found a chance to talk to Koguma today!"'

My mouth dropped open. 'Huh?'

Kazama looked down, her face reddening. 'I – well – I've had a crush on you for ages,' she said. 'To be honest, I don't actually have anything to ask your opinion about today, either. It was just an excuse.'

To my utter shock, Kazama turned out to have had a thing for me ever since we'd started working together. But I'd always assumed she had a boyfriend, because she was so cute, and so good-natured that she brightened up the whole branch.

When I asked if she wouldn't prefer someone better-looking as a boyfriend, she said, 'I like people who seem kind. And the way you look makes me feel safe.'

So that was why she'd suspected Takada might have been covering up a crush. I had no idea there were women who actually preferred men who looked like me. So much was happening today I was struggling to keep up.

But her directness in conveying her feelings deserved a sincere reply.

'The truth is, up until now I've always hated the way I look,' I said. 'And I'm still not sure how to deal with women and love and so on. So . . . is it okay if we start as friends?'

My heart was pounding so hard I thought it might burst out of my chest. The old me would never have dreamed of delivering a line like that.

I'd always thought of my life as an appendage to someone else's. It took my boss and Kazama to teach me that this wasn't the case.

Kazama blushed again. 'Of course,' she said with a smile.

That night, I threw away the other box of *wasanbon*.

Ironic as it was, my brief period of invisibility had taught me how much the people in my life actually noticed and appreciated me.

Was Kogetsu really a kami? If I went back to the shrine, would the Amberglow Candy Store still be there behind it?

But I had no interest in going back to find out. Sometimes ignorance was bliss.

*

Outside a certain two-storey apartment building, with a clear view of a certain balcony, a figure in *hakama* trousers stood atop the property's high surrounding wall, silhouetted against the moon.

Kogetsu twitched his fox ears and swished his tail. 'How perceptive women are,' he murmured. 'Koguma didn't even notice, but Kazama saw it at once: Takada *did* return his feelings, and what she said in junior high school was simply to hide her embarrassment.'

His golden eyes narrowed as his mouth curved into a smile.

'If Koguma had let Takada finish what she meant to say in that apartment, an entirely different fate may have awaited them. But if both are happy now, I suppose things worked out for the best.'

Kogetsu reached out his hand and made a beckoning gesture. The *wasanbon* Koguma had thrown away appeared before him. He exhaled on the cherry-blossom-shaped sweets and encased them in an amber glow.

'Another fascinating sample,' he said. 'And

imagine thinking I was a kami! Humans entertain the oddest of notions.'

Kogetsu saw movement in the apartment behind the balcony: a rotund human form, just barely discernible through the curtains. He watched as the lights in the room went out, and then disappeared from sight.

CHAPTER 3

All-Is-Revealed Chestnut Monaka

Things I like: cats, photography, TV shows about love and romance, tea with milk. Oh, and anything sweet, but especially fruit sandwiches. Some people reject fruit on bread, but the balance between fresh fruit and the hint of saltiness in bread is exactly why it works so well.

But I'd never told my friends any of this. They didn't know that I loved tuxedo cats in particular, or enjoyed shooting with toy cameras.

I might have mentioned my fondness for tea with milk, but I wouldn't have bothered telling them my favourite tea-leaf company. It would have felt like derailing a casual chat about a popular TV show by bringing up some obscure series from overseas. When you went off on obscure tangents that didn't interest anybody else, things got awkward.

I couldn't always tell where the line between small talk and deeper conversation lay. And when I wasn't sure, I stopped talking. It was easier to switch to listen-and-nod mode.

My friends at university liked to tease me about drifting off into my own world or zoning out mid-conversation. But the truth was, most of the time I just couldn't find the words to go with the flow.

And, to be honest, I didn't always *want* to. Sometimes I fantasized about speaking my mind – opening up about my deepest feelings. But I didn't know if my friends would want that. So when they said, 'Yui, you're so quiet,' all I could do was offer an ambiguous smile.

*

The day it all began, I arrived at university for a first-period class. My friends were waving at me from across the lecture hall.

'Yui! Over here!'

I took the seat they had saved for me, and greeted them with a cheerful 'Good morning!'

'Morning, Yui! I love your outfit – that striped top and flared skirt look really cute together!'

This was Saya, our gorgeous fashionista with her wavy chestnut hair.

'Morning. You didn't forget anything today?'

My other friend was Reo. She was also beautiful, but in a more elegant, timeless way, with short black hair and a distinct boyish style.

The three of us were completely different in appearance and personality, but for some reason when we met we just clicked, and quickly became great friends.

In terms of fashion, I was completely average compared to them – your basic, default university student. I envied how they'd already found flattering ways to dress and make themselves up. We were all the same age, but I didn't wear make-up in high school, so I was still figuring it out as I went along. I wasn't used to choosing my own clothes every day after so many years wearing school uniforms, either, so all my outfits were pretty similar. Sometimes I wished I could magically clothe myself in looks right out of magazines instead.

Saya always spoke her mind, sometimes a little

sharply. Conversely, Reo didn't talk about herself much, but she was a good listener. And I was the space cadet in the group that the other two loved to tease.

Our little friend group had a good thing going. But lately, as summer break approached, things had started to change.

Around three months into the school year, just as we'd finally got used to our lectures and the freedom of university life and were finding our places in the campus community, Saya had found herself a boyfriend. He was a couple of years ahead of us; she'd met him in the university tennis club. So far, so good – but then Saya started to change. She couldn't let a day go by without bragging about him.

At first, it was heartwarming to hear her talk about her boyfriend, because it was clear she really liked him. She told us about the surprise gift he got her for their one-month anniversary, and the time he took her on a date to the restaurant everyone had been talking about.

But at some point – it was hard to say when, exactly – her bragging had started to take on a different tone.

'Yui, you really need a more sophisticated look if you want to find a boyfriend,' she'd say. 'You too, Reo – you have to think a little bit more about what guys like when you plan your outfits!'

When she told us about a friend of hers in tennis club dating a boy in our year, she added, 'Older guys are way better though, right? First-years don't have cars yet, they don't have any money – they're just not in the running.'

It was like she always had to add a sentence or two to put the people around her down.

Her warnings about my dating prospects always left me with a vague nagging feeling in my chest. I didn't feel the need for a boyfriend at that point, so I resented the implication that it was some kind of universal goal.

Around that time, I happened to watch a new television series about a group of female frenemies who were constantly trying to one-up each other. Watching them belittle one another, I realized with shock that they reminded me of Saya. Was this what she was doing with her remarks? It explained why they nagged at me more and more, even though I always laughed them off in the moment.

But I couldn't tell Saya to stop trying to one-up us, or that I didn't want to hear about her boyfriend anymore. I had the feeling that doing so would destroy the relationship the three of us shared. I was the quiet one who didn't usually share her own opinions, so if I said something that confrontational, they might decide I wasn't who they thought I was and pull away. If I'd been the type of person who made it clear what they liked and didn't like to begin with, would things have been different?

Things might have been easier if I'd been able to talk it over with Reo, but whenever Saya started her bragging, Reo went quiet and ignored her, so I had no idea how she felt about it. All I could do was brood over it on my own.

They were the first friends I'd made on campus. Both of them had things I lacked, and I respected and appreciated them. I would have liked us to get even closer and share how we really felt about things, but it wasn't working out that way. I wasn't even confident that they valued my friendship as much as I valued theirs.

*

After lectures were over for the day, they invited me to hang out with them, but I turned them down. I'd heard rumours that there was a stray cat living in a run-down old shrine not far from campus, and I wanted to check it out. As a cat-loving amateur photographer, there was no way I was going to miss a shot like that. I wouldn't turn down the chance to pet the cat, either.

The shrine was at the top of a small hill. I climbed the stone staircase, walked through the torii gate, and approached the building. As I looked around for any sign of my subject, a black cat emerged unhurriedly from under the building's eaves.

'Aww! You're so cute!' I said.

The cat had big round yellow eyes. It padded closer, meowing like a child demanding attention. I crouched down to pet it for a while, then remembered with a start that I was here to take its photograph.

Black cats usually came out so dark in photographs that you couldn't make out their facial features. One way to prevent this was to add more light to the shot, preferably natural. It was evening now, so there wasn't much bright light available.

At least the orange sky would make a striking backdrop.

But the cat had apparently lost interest in me, because it turned and strolled away.

'Wait!' I said. 'Come back!' I tried clicking my tongue, but the cat only shot me a single backward glance and continued walking towards the back of the shrine precinct.

I chased after the cat, just in time to see it slip into a wide gap in the ring of forest surrounding the shrine.

'What is that . . . ?'

My curiosity piqued, I walked closer to the gap and saw that it led to a long, straight road that stretched directly away from the shrine, lined on both sides with run-down old buildings.

'Huh . . . ?'

It was obviously a shopping street. I'd thought I'd learned everything there was to learn about the streets around campus in the months since enrolling, but clearly not. In fact, I'd never even heard of a shopping street around here.

'Did the cat go in there . . . ?'

The street was completely deserted and utterly

silent. I'd heard about 'shuttered streets' like this, where all the stores had gone out of business as the neighbourhood changed. Either way, a photograph of the cat against those retro buildings would look great.

I decided to venture in. If I did find any cool stores here, I could come back with Saya and Reo at some point.

But my initial excitement at discovering a retro, moody lane cooled quickly.

It was an unsettling place, and not just because of all those drawn shutters. Not all the signs were in Japanese – I couldn't even tell what some of the stores sold. There were no streetlights, just red and white lanterns hanging everywhere, which added to the eerie mood.

Amid all the traditional Japanese-style buildings on the street, a photography studio caught my eye, standing out for its old-fashioned Western-style facade. The display window facing the street was filled with sepia-coloured photographs. Probably an exhibition of old photographs or something.

'Let me see . . .'

When I leaned in for a closer look, I noticed

something odd. All the people in the photographs were wearing costumes. Some had fox or cat ears, and one was wearing a full-body *kappa* costume. All of them were dressed in kimono, sometimes also with *hakama* trousers. I was pretty sure Hallowe'en hadn't reached Japan back when those clothes were the norm, so what kind of event *was* preserved here?

I decided to go in and ask the studio's owner, but when I tried the door it didn't budge.

Meanwhile, the cat I'd been looking for was nowhere to be found. Eventually I reached the T-junction at the end of the shopping street without finding the cat or any particularly photogenic stores.

But maybe that was a lucky thing. Because at the very end of the street I stumbled upon a lovely-looking building with a sign that read AMBERGLOW CANDY STORE.

'This might be more my style,' I said.

From the designs on the door – basically Japanese, but with a hint of Chinese influence here and there – to the pink lantern on a stand outside, the store's exterior conveyed the good taste of its proprietor. Not to mention the fact that it was to be closed 'at the new and full moon'. I loved stores with distinctive concepts like this.

Best of all, the light spilling from within suggested it was open for business. Filled with anticipation, I opened the door.

'Welcome.' A cool voice emerged from the gloom at the rear of the store, and its owner soon followed. I was shocked by how good-looking he was.

Silky blond hair. Golden eyes. Dark *hakama* trousers. Eccentric fashion choices, maybe, but mysteriously apt for the atmosphere inside the store. I'd never seen someone with golden eyes before – coloured contacts, maybe? But his hair was clear and bright all the way to the roots, with no sign of any kind of dye job.

'Hello,' I said.

It was a relief to see that he was so young, and that most of his wares were simple *wagashi* and retro snacks. I'd briefly worried that the place might sell the kind of luxury confectionery beyond the means of a young college student, but even I could afford to shop here. I really should have considered that before coming inside, of course.

'I am Kogetsu, the proprietor of this establishment,' he said, bowing politely. 'Please feel free to look around.'

'Er – right.'

At first I was distracted by the mysterious and handsome Kogetsu – who, for some reason, kept his distance – but the sweets on display soon captured my full attention.

Daifuku, yokan, manju . . . They all looked delicious. Why was it that the moment you saw a sweet treat you realized it was exactly what you wanted? I found myself suddenly fighting off a full-body sugar craving.

I noticed that everything the store sold had a strange name. CRAVING-MORE KONPEITO, INVISIBLE WASANBON . . . I'd never seen names like this for sweets. I wasn't sure why Kogetsu did things this way, but the fanciful feel matched the store's atmosphere.

I walked through the store reading these names with pleasure, but the confection I stopped and instinctively picked up was called ALL-IS-REVEALED CHESTNUT MONAKA.

'All-is-revealed?' I murmured to myself. 'What does that mean?'

'A chestnut might be hidden within a *monaka*'s wafer shell,' Kogetsu immediately replied from across the room, making me jump. 'But some things are better not hidden at all.'

I was a little embarrassed that he'd overheard me talking to myself, but I couldn't help noticing that he was even further away than before.

The long-distance customer service made me vaguely uneasy. Wondering if it was a body-odour issue, I sniffed at one arm, but all I smelled was soap and deodorant.

'Um . . . Why are you all the way over there?' I asked.

'I startled a previous customer by drawing too close. I thought keeping my distance would be safer. Is this unusual to you?' Kogetsu tilted his head. He seemed genuinely curious, as if he didn't realize how strangely he was acting.

'It is a little . . . jarring. Not just being observed from a distance, but also the way you heard me talking to myself.'

'I see. Finding the appropriate distance to put humans at ease is rather challenging.'

Apparently, he had trouble knowing how far

to take things. I envied the boldness of his experimentation, to be honest, given the difficulties I was currently having finding the appropriate distance from my friends.

In any case, I was amused by the idea of chestnut *monaka* that spoke of 'revealing all'.

'I'll take this, please,' I said, carrying a box of three *monaka* to the counter. Kogetsu rang up the purchase on an old-fashioned mechanical register and put my sweets in a sepia paper bag.

'Thank you very much,' he said. 'And please be sure to observe the guidelines for usage . . . and dosage.'

*

I never did find that cat, and I completely forgot to take any photographs of the shopping street. When I got back to my apartment, where I lived alone, the only thing I had to show for my afternoon was the chestnut *monaka*. Admittedly they did look delicious.

The next morning, I ate one of them instead of my usual breakfast. It was even better than it looked: its wafer shell was nice and crunchy, and the chestnut inside was impressively large. I also appreciated that the sweet filling was *tsubu-an*, azuki beans boiled and sweetened but otherwise left whole, instead of mashed white bean or chestnut paste.

On the way to my first lecture of the day, I ran into Saya at the entrance to campus. We exchanged good mornings and walked the rest of the way together.

'Is it hot today or what?' Saya asked, mopping the sweat from her brow.

Somehow, she was even more beautiful than usual. Her skin was glowing, and her eyeshadow and lipstick were both of more mature shades than those she ordinarily applied. She was also wearing a sleeveless top, which was uncommon for her – she always got cold in the air-conditioned lecture halls. Her skirt was asymmetrical, with a low hem that nicely balanced out her daringly exposed shoulders. I could never pull a combination like that off – not that it would occur to me in the first place.

Why go to all this effort? Maybe she had a date tonight? Before I knew it, I was blurting out, 'Saya, you look great today – your make-up and your outfit are so mature and appealing. Do you have a date with your boyfriend?'

Saya's eyes went wide. 'I didn't think you'd notice the change, Yui!' she said. 'You never have before.'

I made a noncommittal noise. The truth was, I had noticed. I'd just never said anything. I wasn't sure it was my place to offer an opinion on the personal styling of the group's acknowledged fashionista.

'But won't you be cold in the lecture hall with bare shoulders?' I asked, my thoughts slipping right out of my mouth again. I usually needed a moment or two to frame my thoughts into words.

'Yep – but not to worry, I brought this cardigan!' Saya replied, showing me a thin off-white cardigan she had in her bag.

'Oh, okay,' I said, relieved. 'No problem, then.'

Saya gave me a quick hug. 'Thank you for noticing!' she said. 'I am going for a more mature look today. I was a little nervous, but I feel a lot more confident now that I know you like it.'

'Huh?' This time I was wide-eyed. 'Me liking it gives you confidence?' Wasn't she always saying that my style was too plain and unsophisticated?

'Of course it does!' Saya said. 'Girlfriends are much harsher judges of these things than boyfriends! Boys don't look that closely. They only notice whether make-up is heavy or light.'

Despite this griping, it was adorable the way she dressed up for her dates. Even if the finer details would be lost on her boyfriend, she still wanted to look her cutest. I might not have had a boyfriend myself, but I understood the impulse.

'So you don't think this new eyeshadow and lipstick are too bold?' Saya asked. 'My make-up did end up a little heavier than I planned . . .'

'Well, they are darker than your usual shades, but I think they suit you. I like it.'

'Great! Now if my boyfriend says my makeup's too heavy, I can tell him, "Well, my friend liked it, and that's enough for me!"'

Saya looked genuinely gleeful as she hugged me again and laughed.

I felt a kind of catch in my chest release. I hadn't even been aware of it before, but now that it was gone, it was as if a pleasant breeze had run through me.

It was good that I'd spoken frankly. It was

good that I'd complimented Saya instead of hesitating, even though I wasn't sure my opinion was worth anything to her. After all, no one minds a compliment.

Still marvelling at Saya's unexpected reaction, I resolved to put my feelings into words in future.

We met up with Reo for our first lecture, and soon the morning's classes were over. Instead of buying lunch at the convenience store on campus, as we did sometimes, we decided to eat in the cafeteria.

While we waited in line for the food ticket machine, Reo looked torn. 'I can't decide between hot and cold udon noodles,' she said at last. This was unusual for her – she usually made decisions quickly and firmly.

'Wouldn't the hot noodles be better, to warm you up? You're having stomach pains, right?'

I realized that the words were coming out of my mouth as soon as I thought them again. Reo gaped at me.

'Uh,' I said, fumbling for an explanation. 'I mean –'

'No, you're right,' Reo said, still looking amazed.

'I have cramps today. I'm impressed that you could tell.'

'W-well,' I stammered, 'I saw you secretly taking painkillers in class, and you look a little pale, so . . .'

As I was struggling to explain myself, Saya grabbed my shoulders from behind and hooked her chin over one of them.

'Yui! Since when do you notice stuff like that? What's got into you today?'

'I don't know,' I admitted.

I really didn't. What *had* got into me today? It was like my mouth had a mind of its own.

Reo noticed me frowning in contemplation and shot me a kind smile. She didn't smile like that very often, and it made my heart beat a little faster.

'I think I will have the hot noodles, just like you suggested, Yui,' she said. 'Thanks for looking out for me.'

'No problem,' I said. But I was distracted, because I was remembering the chestnut *monaka* I'd eaten that morning.

Along with Kogetsu's words: *A chestnut might be hidden within a* monaka*'s wafer shell, but some things are better not hidden at all.*

What if these *monaka* were called 'all-is-revealed' because eating one temporarily prevented you from hiding your true feelings? Maybe that was why I was acting so strange.

After we ordered and received our food, the three of us headed together towards a table. Saya seemed to be smiling more than usual, and even Reo's voice had a hint of good cheer. Was it because I'd changed?

Even if it was the chestnut *monaka* affecting me, it wasn't like those effects were bad. I kept saying things that I usually would have kept to myself, unsure if anyone wanted to hear them – and they loved it.

In which case, whatever the cause, would it be so bad to just go with it? I didn't think it would last that long, anyway. I couldn't explain why, but I had the feeling that when I woke up the next morning I'd be my usual self again.

So why not think of myself as someone else for the day, and enjoy it?

Once that was resolved, I realized I was famished. I got started on my lunch.

*

After a day of lectures, the three of us reconvened at the cafeteria for dinner. Saya's boyfriend had cancelled on her, and she was not happy.

'I got all dressed up, tried something new with my make-up, and look what happens!' she grumbled. She'd been complaining since the cancellation.

'You go on dates every weekend,' Reo said coolly, sipping her iced tea. 'What's the big deal?'

This didn't make Saya feel better. 'I've been looking forward to it since I got up this morning! Can you believe he did this? It reminds me of the other day . . .'

She was off, rehearsing another recent complaint. Reo and I had both heard it many times before. Normally we'd just let her retell the story. But today felt different.

'But, Saya,' I said, 'didn't you tell us that last time when he suddenly cancelled on you, he surprised you with a gift to make up for it? I'm sure he'll make this time up to you, too.'

The other two stared at me in astonishment. I'd actually interrupted Saya's complaining to comfort her.

'Yeah, okay,' Saya said slowly. 'Maybe you're right.'

At first I was relieved that she'd been so easy to convince. But then she started bragging about her boyfriend. It was better than listening to her complain, but we'd heard the boasts over and over again so many times it was hard to know how to respond.

'Both of you need to hurry up and find boyfriends!'

There it was – her standard line. I heard Reo sigh beside me.

Now that I thought about it, Reo did tend to make an irritated face when Saya started gushing about her boyfriend. The sighing was familiar, too. She probably didn't enjoy Saya going on about her love life all the time.

'Huh?' Reo turned to look at me, eyes wide with shock.

'Ex*cuse* me?' Saya said, her voice suddenly lower in pitch. She looked back and forth between Reo and me. 'What was that about?'

Apparently, I'd unwittingly spoken my mind again. And at a particularly delicate moment.

'Um – I didn't – you see –'

I tried to deny it, but it was no good. Saya leaned forward over the table towards Reo.

'Does my boyfriend talk really bother you that much?' she asked.

I watched the two of them anxiously. Then Reo nodded.

'That's right,' Reo said.

'Wha—?!'

Saya was lost for words at first. Reo's attitude must have taken her by surprise. But then I saw anger growing on Saya's face. I'd blabbed too much, and my two friends were about to fight.

'Wait!' I said. 'Let's all calm down for a moment.'

But interposing myself between them, unsurprisingly, only made them turn their baleful glares on me.

'And whose fault *was* this argument, hmm?' Saya asked, crossing her arms and raising one eyebrow.

Reo's expression was hard, too. She was seriously angry. And who could blame her?

'I'm . . . I'm sorry,' I said. 'Anyone want a chestnut *monaka*? They're really tasty.'

I pulled out the box I'd shoved into my bag that morning, as a snack in case I got hungry, and placed it on the table. But changing the subject was worth more than that.

'There's only two left,' Saya grumbled.

'I already had one, this morning,' I said. 'You two can have these.'

Making sure to smile, I held the box out to Saya. The prickly atmosphere between the two of us eased a little.

'Well, I was feeling peckish for something sweet,' Saya admitted. 'I guess I won't say no.'

'Me neither,' said Reo.

Each of them took a *monaka* and bit into it.

'Hey, this is delicious!'

'Mmm. This *anko* is perfect – not too bland, not too sweet.'

I was relieved to see that the mood seemed to be improving.

Then Saya tilted her head, looking puzzled. 'Wait, didn't you say these were chestnut *monaka*?' she asked. 'Mine doesn't have a chestnut.'

'Neither does mine,' said Reo.

'Really? That's weird,' I said. 'The one I ate this morning definitely did.'

The two of them held up their half-eaten *monaka* to show me. They were right. Both were filled with sweetened beans, but neither had a chestnut. And after I'd been so impressed by how big the chestnut was in mine, too.

'Yui, are you sure you didn't buy regular *monaka* by mistake?'

'Classic Yui, if so.'

'Maybe . . . ?' I said slowly.

I could easily have made that mistake if I'd picked up three individual *monaka*, but this was supposed to be a triple-pack of the chestnut kind. Had Kogetsu made a mistake when boxing them up?

After finishing her *monaka* and taking a sip of her iced tea, Reo said, 'To get back to what we were talking about before – to be honest, I don't feel the need for a boyfriend right now. I'm enjoying my classes here, and working at my part-time job and hanging out with my friends feels more meaning-ful to me. So I'm getting sick of you talking about your boyfriend every time we meet up, and telling us we need to get boyfriends of our own.'

After this came out in a rush, she looked away slowly, not meeting Saya's gaze.

'I wasn't planning to say all that, though,' she said quietly.

'I can't believe you!' Saya said. She leaned over the table, furious, but I took her arm to hold her back.

'Saya,' I said. 'Calm down.'

Was the power of the chestnut *monaka* working on Reo, too? Anyone who ate one seemed to become incapable of hiding their true feelings. If so, then maybe Saya was also about to –

'It's not like I *want* to talk about my boyfriend all the time!' Saya said.

A brief silence. 'Huh?' I said.

I'd been worried that the discussion might get even more heated if Saya started showing the chestnut-*monaka* effect, too, but things had taken an unexpected turn.

'I don't have any hobbies or interests like you,' she said to me, and then, turning to Reo, continued, 'and I'm definitely not as secure in my skin as you. Without my boyfriend all I'd be is another boring face in the crowd. That's why I brag about him – it feels like I'm finally ahead of you two at something. I know a boyfriend isn't a possession, but having one makes me feel more worthy.'

Reo and I exchanged a startled look. Our

cheerful, fearless Saya was secretly wracked with insecurity? Really?

'But you seem so confident! You're pretty, you have your own style . . .'

Saya shook her head grimly. 'It's all copied straight out of fashion magazines. And the make-up is from online video tutorials – everything you need to know is just a search away these days. My appearance is just a pastiche of what other people are doing.'

I'd never fathomed she might feel this way.

'But that's still throwing yourself into something you like,' I said. 'It's no different from me and my photography.'

Reo nodded. 'I agree. You shouldn't put yourself down like that. There's no way you could master fashion and make-up like that if you weren't interested in them. I sure haven't.'

'I know, right?' I said. 'Doing your make-up properly every day, curling your hair . . . I couldn't keep it up. You're amazing, Saya.'

'You . . . really think so?'

Saya seemed smaller than usual, uncertainty lacing her eyes. She'd really opened up about her true feelings. I wanted to reciprocate – and as soon as

I felt that urge, my mouth opened of its own accord.

'I don't even *know* your boyfriend,' I said. 'But I like you, and I've always wished you'd talk more about yourself. I've never once thought you were a face in the crowd.'

'Yui . . .' said Saya, tearing up.

Reo flashed a gentle smile. 'I'll cosign that,' she said. 'If you were telling us about yourself, I wouldn't get fed up at all, even if the topic itself didn't interest me.'

Hearing this even made me happy. I felt my eyelids getting hot.

'I'm glad you told us how you feel, Reo,' I said. 'I admire the way you're always so cool and collected, but sometimes it makes me worry that you don't even enjoy spending time with us.'

Reo shook her head. 'I'm not cool at all,' she said. 'I'm just not a good talker, so I learned to be a listener instead. My parents have told me my whole life that I should be more expressive – that they can't tell from my face how I'm feeling.'

'Really?'

At home, I was always being told to pull myself together or to calm down, so I knew what it was like to have your parents on your back. But I had no idea Reo had similar experiences.

'I never would have guessed that, Reo,' I said.

'Me neither!' said Saya. 'I mean, she's been like that since we met. That's just Reo!'

Reo's poker face reddened a little around the cheeks. 'Thanks,' she said. 'And, Yui – please don't ever worry that I don't enjoy spending time with you. I think of you both as close friends who accept me as I am.'

'Uh . . .'

My brain froze at this sudden confession. Fortunately, Saya jumped in.

'Me too!' she cried. 'You're both really special to me, and I care about you just as much as I do my boyfriend! The difference is, it'd be weird to ask friends, "Hey, do you like me?"'

I'd got an answer to the question I was most afraid to ask from both of them at once. But Saya wasn't done.

'Since I had no way to tell how much you liked me, I was worried, too. In the past, my friends have always got fed up with me – they say I'm too strong-willed, or too blunt, or . . .'

Reo patted her on the shoulder. 'If you weren't strong-willed, you wouldn't be our Saya,' she said.

I nodded. 'You're not afraid to say what you mean,' I said. 'I respect that.'

Then it was my turn under the spotlight.

'Yui, I'm sorry I always tease you about zoning out and being a space case,' Reo said. 'The truth is, your kindness is really soothing to me.'

'You might be the reason we get along so well,' Saya said. 'Like a shock absorber for friendship.'

These compliments were so unexpected that I was initially more startled than happy.

'You mean I bring something to the table, too?'

'Obviously you do! Why else would we be this close?'

Saya almost seemed to be pouting. But it seemed that all three of us had somehow lost sight of what should have been 'obvious'.

'In other words,' I said slowly, 'we all feel the same way . . . ?'

Each of us had our own worries and hang-ups, but we all cared about each other, too. I felt my heart grow warmer at the thought.

'I can't believe we were all nervous about the

same thing, even though we're so different,' Saya said. 'That's so funny.'

'Maybe we're more similar than we realize,' Reo said.

She might have hit the mark there. Maybe it was being different in some ways but similar in others that made us such good friends.

Saya leaned back and stretched in her chair. 'I feel sooo much better now that I've got all that out,' she said.

I realized that the vague nagging in my chest was gone, too. 'We should have opened up to each other earlier,' I sighed. 'I don't know why we thought we had to hide all that stuff.'

'I wonder what made it so easy to talk about today,' Reo said, sounding mystified. 'I don't know about you two, but it was like my mouth had a mind of its own.'

'Maybe it was the chestnut *monaka*,' I said quietly, looking at the empty box. But the group at the next table laughed as I spoke, and Yui and Reo didn't hear me.

'Did you say something, Yui?'

'No,' I said. 'It's nothing.'

Whether today's miracle was because of the chestnut *monaka* or not, I resolved never to forget it. From this day on, I wouldn't need any assistance sharing my feelings.

*

A shadowy figure perched atop a tree outside gazed down at the three young women through the cafeteria's tall glass windows.

None of the university's students noticed Kogetsu up there in his *hakama* as they trod the paths between buildings below, as orange evening light streamed from the west.

Kogetsu let the corners of his mouth turn up in a smile.

'Intriguingly enough,' he murmured, 'only the first of those *monaka* contained any mystical power. I completely forgot to imbue the others with it – or to put the chestnuts in. Not intentionally, of course.'

As he spoke, Kogetsu summoned to him the few fragments of *monaka* remaining in the box.

'She believes it was the *monaka* that made today's conversation possible. I suppose the lesson is that speaking truly can induce others to reveal their true selves as well. In any case, I shall take my usual sample.'

The *monaka* fragments, now encased in amber, sat on Kogetsu's hand, reflecting the evening sunlight. One of the students below noticed the glinting from the trees, but by the time they were peering up more closely, Kogetsu was gone.

CHAPTER 4

Surrogate Caramels

When I picked up my shiny brass trumpet, I felt my attention sharpen.

Bringing the mouthpiece to my lips to play the first note, I felt like the instrument and I instantly became one.

The sound of the trumpet seemed to ring out especially well in the autumn air. Why was that, exactly?

I was still pondering this question when I heard Ayaka, the trumpet section leader, call the section together. 'Okay, warmup over,' she said. 'Everyone over here for section practice.'

School was over for the day, and brass band rehearsal had begun. I left the corner of the room where I'd been warming up and joined the other trumpet players gathering by Ayaka.

'We'll start with long tones,' she said, and set the metronome ticking. We all started playing together in time. When Ayaka was first made section leader, she was so nervous that her face was stiff and blank, but now she looked more comfortable in the role. Relaxed, even.

'After this, we'll split up again and everyone can practise the piece for the music festival on their own. We've got a full-band rehearsal after this, so make sure you can play through the whole thing.'

'We will,' we chorused.

Once section practice was over, I went back to the corner of the room where I'd left my music stand. Another member of the trumpet section, an underclassman one year below me, came over and asked if I had a moment.

'Sure,' I said. 'What's up?'

'There's a passage I'm having trouble with,' she said. Trumpet in hand, she leaned over my music stand and pointed at the tricky part on the sheet music. 'Right here?'

'Oh, that bit?' I asked. 'It goes like this . . .' I played the phrase for her.

'Your long notes ring out so well, Risa!' she said, looking at me with admiration.

I couldn't deny that it felt good to be praised.

'Wouldn't you be better off asking Ayaka for advice, though?' I asked. I didn't think so at all, to be honest, but I wanted to hear the response I knew she'd give.

'But you and I were in brass band together in grade school,' she said. 'It's easier to ask you. And, to be honest, I think you're a better player than her . . . Oh – please don't tell the others I said that.'

I nodded. 'Of course,' I said. I couldn't stop myself from grinning, despite feeling a little embarrassed about drawing so much pride and confidence from a younger student's opinion.

I was mediocre at studying, so-so at sports, and my only real hobby was reading. Playing the trumpet was my one opportunity to be best at something.

I'd started playing in grade school, so when I joined the school brass band in junior high, I attracted notice as one of the few members who actually had experience.

But in the second term of my second year, when

all the third-years retired from club activities to concentrate on their high-school entrance exams and the new section leaders were chosen, I wasn't one of them.

Ayaka Takahashi was chosen as trumpet section leader instead. She was in the same year as me, and she'd only started playing in junior high, but she'd improved so rapidly that she was already good enough to play beside me.

I assumed it was her good grades and trustworthy nature that won her the role. In terms of musical skill, I was still the winner. That much I was sure of, but I still felt nervous about falling behind.

The band was currently preparing for the local music festival, which was held every year in autumn. The piece we were going to play had a trumpet solo in it, and there were two candidates for the soloist: Ayaka and me. To decide which one of us got the part, there was going to be a two-person audition.

Ayaka and I would take turns playing the solo, and the rest of the band, along with the teacher advising us, would vote on the winner. If I lost a vote like that, I might never recover.

And I had good reason to think I might lose. Strange as it may sound, I was naturally unlucky.

After practice was over, I visited the shrine near the school to pray for success. Lately I'd been visiting the shrine every day, even though it made my walk home longer. It was a tiny, run-down place, but apparently my parents had taken me there as a baby for my first shrine visit, so it felt like I could trust the kami there somehow.

'Please don't let me mess up at the audition,' I prayed fervently. 'Please protect me from my usual bad luck!'

Even if the kami couldn't turn my luck around completely, even a minor reprieve would help.

I was unlucky in every way you can imagine. Not only did I tend to choke when it really mattered – tripping during the sprint on Sports Day, flubbing notes during important band performances – I was also constantly dealing with minor misfortunes, from riding my bike into lampposts to stepping in dog poop. Sometimes it felt like I was being tormented by a spirit of ill fortune.

In any case, it would literally be just my luck

to mess up that audition. And I really, *really* didn't want to do that.

Ayaka got good grades, the teachers trusted her – she had so much that I didn't. She was a model student, and now she was section leader, too.

But the trumpet was all I had. I couldn't lose my only source of pride to someone who already had everything. To be honest, part of me resented her for even competing for that solo. Couldn't she bow out gracefully and let me have this? But I knew that Ayaka would take the audition as seriously as everything else she did. She would step up and give that solo everything she had.

If only there was some way to ensure I wouldn't mess up. Like temporarily transferring my bad luck to someone else instead. Say . . . Ayaka?

'No, no, no! No thinking like that!'

Shaking my head to banish the idea, I turned and walked away from the main shrine building. That kind of twisted thinking was like losing before the battle had even begun.

Just then I heard a crow cawing from the rear of the shrine grounds, and reflexively glanced back.

It looked the same as ever . . . but for some reason, something seemed off.

'Huh?!'

Before I could give it any thought, I realized why. There was a gap in the trees at the border of the shrine precinct, like a hole in a wall that was meant to keep intruders out.

But why was there a gap? I was pretty sure it wasn't there when I visited yesterday. Had some shrine priest come by to chop a tree down earlier today?

Curious, I walked closer to the grassy gap – only to see something even more surprising beyond it.

A long road, barely surfaced, stretched directly away from the shrine. It was lined on both sides with what looked like stores.

'A shopping street . . . ? But why?'

I'd visited this shrine many times, and I was sure there'd never been a shopping street nearby before. This made no sense. Not to mention the eerie quiet of the place, or the retro buildings completely untouched by modern trends. What kind of commercial district looked like this? One on the verge of closing down, maybe . . .

I shouldn't waste my time here, I thought. *I should hurry home and go over the score for that solo part.* I knew this intellectually, but a strange force seemed to pull at my feet until they were suddenly moving of their own accord.

Nothing inflames adolescent curiosity like a hint of danger, I guess.

By the time I was halfway down the street, one thing was clear to me: none of the stores were open for business. Some had their curtains drawn so I couldn't see in, while others were pitch black inside to begin with. See? I was naturally unlucky.

I also realized this shopping street wasn't just 'retro', as I'd initially thought. Some of the stores had Chinese-style facades. There were lanterns hung everywhere instead of street lights. And some of the signs were in languages I'd never seen before. It was a mysterious combination – a streetscape from some decades-old movie, with a set design borrowed from an even older film from China, plus a few details from fantasy cinema, if that made sense. All lit up by the setting orange sun, it really was like a movie set.

'Ooh – a music store!'

Many of the stores had nothing at all in their windows, but one had musical instruments on display. I hurried happily towards it, but when I got close enough to the window I saw that the instrument I'd thought was a violin was actually something else entirely, even if it did have strings. It reminded me of the one in pictures of the Seven Gods of Fortune, so maybe it was a biwa? I also saw a black wooden flute and a bunch of taiko drums, but not a single instrument from the standard brass-band ensemble.

I figured there'd at least be mouthpieces and reeds inside, so I pushed at the door. It creaked a little, but didn't budge. Would it have killed them to put out their CLOSED sign?

I walked on, disappointed, but I didn't see a single other store that interested me. Not that any of them were open anyway. And then I reached the T-junction at the end of the street.

There I saw a store with a round pink lantern outside it, illuminating a sign that read AMBERGLOW CANDY STORE. It seemed to be open, but I was a little dubious. I mean, what kind of candy store shut down during 'the new and full moon'? And why 'Amberglow'? It sounded kind of New Agey. What if they tried to sell me some weird herbal remedy instead of candy?

Better just go home, I thought again. But then it hit me. If this place *did* sell herbal remedies, maybe they had something that could help counteract my bad luck. Something to ease anxiety, for example.

I decided to peek inside. If I sensed danger, I'd just make a run for it. As a trumpet player, I was pretty confident in my lung capacity.

Slowly, trying not to make a sound, I pushed at the carved wooden door. Once it was half-open, I peered inside and saw . . . a completely normal candy store.

I breathed a sigh of relief and walked in. Some of the shelves had traditional *wagashi* like *wasanbon* and *monaka*, while others had retro snacks like *konpeito*.

As I was roaming the aisles checking everything out, someone emerged from behind the counter.

'My apologies,' he said. 'I was occupied with some work in our back rooms, and failed to notice that we had a customer.'

'N-no problem,' I stammered.

The storekeeper was a blond hottie wearing

hakama, and he stood so close to me, I felt my heart beat faster. I'd never seen a man with such a beautiful face.

'Welcome to the Amberglow Candy Store,' the man said, his golden eyes narrowing as he smiled. 'I am Kogetsu, the proprietor. Please take your time and look around.'

A storekeeper who was polite even to junior-high students. Don't get me wrong – I wasn't letting my guard down just because he was hot, but it also didn't seem likely he was selling anything dangerous. I figured it should be safe to relax and browse the sweets on offer.

All the names on the shelf signs had a strange twist to them. CRAVING-MORE KONPEITO, INVISIBLE WASANBON, ALL-IS-REVEALED CHESTNUT MONAKA . . . Combined with the 'new and full moon' bit and the *hakama*, it added up to a very idiosyncratic establishment.

But I had to admit, the sweets looked delicious.

My eye landed on a box of caramels that made me pause. I was initially drawn to the retro box, which I'd never seen in any other store, but what made me pick it up was the name on the sign.

Surrogate Caramels. I got the uncomfortable feeling that the caramels themselves could sense my earlier thoughts about sticking Ayaka with my bad luck.

'Everyone has some troubles they'd rather force someone else to deal with – don't you find?'

Kogetsu spoke from directly behind me, making me jump.

'You seem to be struggling with certain . . . personal qualities,' he continued. 'Perhaps those caramels could be of use.'

'H-how did you know about that?' I asked. He spoke as if he knew the whole story, from my innate bad luck to my worries about the upcoming audition.

'Just a hunch,' he said.

'A hunch . . . ?'

I suppose it was fair to assume that anyone who picked up a box of 'Surrogate Caramels' had issues they'd rather make someone else's problem.

Not that I really believed the caramels had that kind of power. Still, they were cheap enough that I bought a pack. I liked caramels, and the box really was cute.

Kogetsu rang up the purchase on a mechanical cash register and carefully put my caramels into a sepia paper bag.

'Oh, you didn't have to – but thanks.'

Kogetsu bowed his head low. But I still saw the corners of his mouth twitch.

'Thank you for your purchase,' he said. 'And do be careful. These caramels can become quite habit-forming – like a sticky sweetness that lingers in the mouth.'

*

'Wow. That *is* sweet.'

After dinner that night, I tried one of the caramels. The sweetness was so intense it made my throat burn.

I hadn't had a caramel in a long time – was this normal? It felt like the whole inside of my mouth was sticky with it.

Half-choking, I went to the kitchen for some water, which finally brought relief.

I cleared my throat. 'Still, that sweetness might not be all bad . . .'

I was wide awake now, for one thing. Maybe I could save these caramels for studying before exams.

The following morning, I tossed a caramel into my mouth before leaving the house. And that's when things got strange.

The first sign came when I arrived at school, joining the stream of uniformed students shuffling towards the gates. I heard a shriek from behind me, and when I turned to look I saw a girl holding one foot off the ground and grimacing in disgust.

'I can't believe this!' she cried. 'I just washed these sneakers – why did I have to step in dog poop!'

A second girl, evidently a friend, watched with pity in her eyes as the first scraped her shoe on the sidewalk. 'Yikes,' she said. 'Don't let it get to you, I guess.'

Normally, I would have been the star of that particular tragedy. Today, however, it seemed I'd steered around the dog poop without even realizing.

I guess I do get lucky sometimes, I thought, but that was as far as it went then.

*

In fourth period, I started to sense that something really was off.

It was just before lunch, so I was too hungry to do anything but stare into space.

'Now, who can solve the next problem . . . ?'

I glanced at our maths teacher, standing at the blackboard by a freshly written equation, and braced myself for the usual call. *Okay, Saito,* our teacher would say, *you're up*. But then –

'Okay, Sai—I mean, Watanabe,' our teacher said, his gaze smoothly shifting from me to Watanabe instead.

'Huh?' Watanabe scrambled for his textbook. He'd clearly assumed I would be called on and settled back to watch.

A friend who sat one row behind me poked my shoulder. 'Was that lucky or what?' she said.

'I guess so . . .'

My friends knew how unlucky I was. Under normal circumstances, I would be in the hot seat right now, not Watanabe.

Not that I was complaining. Maths wasn't my best subject, and I had no idea how to solve the question on the board. But I did wonder why our teacher had started to say my name before switching to Watanabe's instead.

Surrogate Caramels. The name ran through my head again.

What if that girl from this morning and Watanabe had been surrogates for my misfortune? What if I really could force other people to bear my bad luck now?

The sweet taste of the caramel from this morning came back to me. I gulped.

If I was right, I didn't have to be naturally unlucky anymore. I'd be sure to win the solo. As long as someone else got the bad luck instead . . .

It wasn't like I was asking them to bear my bad luck for the rest of their lives – only for the duration of the audition. Was that so awful? Given how unlucky my life had been, couldn't I be allowed that much?

I pretended not to notice how guilty I felt as I rehearsed these self-justifications, or the pricking sensation in my chest.

As the audition approached, I kept eating one caramel a day to make sure I didn't have an accident and injure myself.

Strangely enough, the sticky sweetness seemed stronger every time.

Previously, I would have got in trouble for forgetting a textbook, or frantically tried to salvage a failed science class experiment, but none of that happened anymore. My mistakes were being made by other classmates.

My parents made a point to tell me how impressed they were by my newfound composure after always having been so careless about things. My friends were amazed, too, asking why I was on such a roll lately.

But I took no pleasure watching other people make the mistakes I used to. It only underscored how tough my old life had been. The prospect of going back to that after the audition was frightening. Could I really give up these caramels?

*

Soon it was the day of the audition.

It was on a Saturday, so we had an all-day band rehearsal in lieu of classes. The audition was held in the evening as a kind of grand finale.

When the time came, everyone arranged their chairs in the music room the same way they did for full-band performances, but then sat down to face the back of the room. They would decide between our performances without knowing whose was whose.

Ayaka and I decided by lot that she would play first. I went to wait outside the room and did my best not to listen to her performance, but the room's soundproofing wasn't enough to muffle her trumpet completely.

She was hitting some beautiful high notes, as usual, but she was also making mistakes. If I could get through the solo without any mistakes of my own, I could beat her. My tone might not have been as lovely as hers, but the teacher who supervised brass band had told me before that I was better than Ayaka in other areas: confidence, for example, and the way my crisp tone went straight out to the audience. All I had to do was play up those strengths in my audition.

When my turn came, performing while everyone had their backs turned felt strange, but I played even better than I had during practice, making no mistakes at all. Even the high notes where my pitch usually slipped came out perfectly. By the second half of the solo I was actually enjoying myself.

See? I thought. *When I get the chance to show what I can really do, look how well I can play!* I'd never had that kind of chance before, so I'd always been unfairly compared to Ayaka – but this audition proved that she wasn't even in my league.

My performance won the vote two to one. The solo part was mine.

As the other band members applauded, I sneaked a glance at Ayaka. She was biting her lip and seemed to be holding back tears.

After practice, my adoring underclassman came over to me.

'Congratulations!' she said, not bothering to lower her voice. I winced and looked around, but Ayaka didn't seem to be in the room anymore.

'Thanks,' I said.

'Your audition was amazing! Not a single mistake!'

'Yeah, I managed to keep my nerves under control.'

Thanks to the caramels, sure – but they'd only

given me a chance to show what I was truly capable of.

'I felt a little sorry for Ayaka,' the other girl continued. 'Every mistake she made seemed to throw
her off more.'

I still didn't feel any guilt, but my heart did give
an unpleasant *thump* at that.

'Oh, really?' I said. 'I wasn't paying attention.'

'She doesn't usually mess up like that. Do you
think she got stage fright?'

I hesitated. 'Maybe so,' I said at last. But my
mind was already going in other directions.

Had my surrogate today been Ayaka?

Had my error-free performance been at her
expense, preventing her from showing what *she*
could really do?

My underclassman must have noticed the horror
on my face, because she quickly added, 'That's not
your problem, of course! It's no wonder you're
better under pressure – you've had more experience, right back to grade school.'

'I guess so,' I said.

Maybe I was overthinking it. Even if Ayaka hadn't
been my surrogate, everyone made mistakes when

they got nervous. Why should she be an exception?

I packed my trumpet in its case, and went into the storage room to put it away. Before I could, though, I heard voices. There were two of them – and one was crying. Startled, I hid behind a shelf.

'Too bad about the audition, Ayaka,' said one of the voices.

'Yeah . . .'

I peeked cautiously around the corner. There was Ayaka, crouched in the corner and crying. One of her friends, a trombone player in our year, was trying to comfort her.

'What happened, though?' Ayaka's friend asked. 'You played that solo so well in rehearsals.'

'I don't know!' Ayaka wailed. 'Why did I have to mess up on the big day? I practised and practised to make sure I wouldn't get nervous, but when I started playing, my mind went blank!'

Every word Ayaka forced out through her sobs seemed to grab me by the chest.

If not for those caramels, I might have been where she was right now.

'I remember how hard you worked for it,' Ayaka's friend said. 'You even came in early before school and got our club advisor to open the music room on days with no rehearsal, all so you could get in some extra practice.'

Extra practice? This was the first I'd heard of this. My trumpet case shook as my hands started to tremble.

'I guess I made you come in early with me every morning for nothing,' Ayaka said. 'Sorry about that.'

'Don't be silly!' the other girl said. 'I didn't mind at all.'

I heard Ayaka get to her feet and the two of them started walking my way, so I rushed out of the storage room before they could catch me eavesdropping.

The underclassman from earlier was still in the music room outside. She looked at the trumpet case in my hand, puzzled. 'I thought you went to put that away,' she said.

My heart was pounding so frantically, and I was having such trouble breathing, that I couldn't answer.

I had no idea that Ayaka was practising before school every morning. Or after school, on days when there was no rehearsal. The other trumpet players hadn't mentioned it, which probably meant that only our club advisor and Ayaka's close friends knew.

Everyone gets nervous during a big performance: I hadn't even questioned this assumption. But it was wrong.

My history of messing up on stage was simply because I didn't practise enough. If I wasn't ironing out problems during practice, how could I expect them to disappear on the big day?

Ayaka was putting in multiple times the effort I was, specifically to avoid that.

On school mornings, I slept in as long as I could. On days with no club rehearsal, I happily went home to laze around. But not Ayaka. She'd been practising. Quietly, without making a big deal out of it.

And then, after working so hard to eliminate any chance of mistakes, she'd been forced to make *my* mistakes instead.

'I think I might have done something I can't take back,' I said, and sat down heavily on the ground. I heard the underclassman – my biggest fan – getting flustered above me, but I didn't have time to worry about that.

For the next week, I didn't eat any caramels. Instead, I observed myself as closely as I could. It was an eye-opening experience.

For example, I *was* constantly stepping in dog poop and tripping over on the way to school, but only because I didn't look where I was going. And *that* was because I left the house so late that I didn't have time to watch the road carefully.

Teachers *did* call on me in class a lot, but only when I was gazing blankly out the window – or looking down at my lap, pretending not to notice their gaze, desperately praying they'd pick someone else.

My science experiments and home-ec recipes *did* tend to fail, but only because I was sloppy about measurements and careless about procedure.

I'd always thought of myself as naturally unlucky, but in fact I wasn't at all.

There was no mystery. The bad luck was my fault. I was careless, inattentive and easily distracted. End of story.

Kogetsu's words came back to me.

You seem to be struggling with certain . . . personal qualities.

He'd only mentioned 'personal qualities', not my 'nature'. He must have seen through me right from the start, recognizing me as a cocky junior-high student who used the idea of being naturally unlucky as a convenient excuse for ignoring her own flaws.

I'd abstained from eating the caramels since the day of the audition, but I could still feel that sticky sweetness in my mouth. I realized now that it was guilt – guilt over making Ayaka fail in front of the whole band, even though she'd done nothing to deserve it.

I couldn't turn back time or change history so the audition had never happened. But there was one way I could redeem myself – something no one could do but me.

*

'Excuse me, Ms Hasegawa. Do you have a moment?'

It was lunchtime, and I was at the school staff room, talking to our club advisor.

'Saito?' she said, raising her eyebrows. 'We don't see you here very often. To what do I owe the pleasure?'

Some students – the kind who got good

grades – visited the staff room regularly to ask the teachers questions about what they were studying in class, but I wasn't that proactive. Other students visited on school club business – for example, the president and vice president of the brass band club came here to get the key to the music room, and section leaders came to discuss practice plans with Ms Hasegawa. Again, I wasn't in either group.

As a result, I hardly ever visited the staff room, and I felt deeply out of place there. Unlike our classrooms, it was filled with grown-ups. Noticing me looking around and fidgeting, Ms Hasegawa gently said, 'Did you have something you wanted to discuss?'

'Yes.' I cleared my throat. 'It's about the trumpet solo.'

'The part you won last week? Are you having trouble with phrasing?'

'No, that's not it.' I took a deep breath and said the words I'd been practising in my head since the morning: 'I'm not happy with how the audition worked out. Could we please redo it?'

Ms Hasegawa's eyes widened for a moment. Then her expression grew thoughtful. 'Are you sure about this?'

'Yes. Ayaka's playing wasn't at its best that day. I'm sure you noticed.'

On the other hand, *my* playing was better than it had any right to be. I didn't say this aloud, but I got the sense that she felt the same way.

'Being able to perform even when put on the spot, and staying healthy to make that possible, are also skills a musician needs,' Ms Hasegawa said. 'Are you taking that into account, too?'

'Yes,' I said. 'Of course.'

Ms Hasegawa studied my expression. I met her gaze and said nothing. When she saw that I wasn't going to change my mind, her face softened and she let out a sigh. 'All right,' she said. 'Let me think about this. I'll make my decision by today's rehearsal.'

'Thank you,' I said, and I meant it. I bowed deeply and realized with shock that it might have been the first time I'd ever made such a sincere bow to an adult.

'I must say, I didn't expect *you* to come to me about this,' Ms Hasegawa said. 'Junior-high students grow up so quickly.'

She smiled and looked off into the distance.

*

At our pre-rehearsal club meeting that day, when Ms Hasegawa announced that Ayaka and I would be redoing the audition – at my request – the room boiled over with shocked voices.

The younger girl who'd been in elementary school with me looked my way like a pigeon pinged with a peashooter. Ayaka looked frozen in her chair.

I followed Ayaka's lead and sat quietly, facing straight ahead, without saying anything to anyone. I realized I actually liked who I was at this moment. I'd never felt this way before.

*

The audition do-over was held the following Saturday. It was no contest. Ayaka's performance was elegant and assured, showcasing her signature beautiful tone and rich vibrato. I'd thought I'd done pretty well during the first audition, but her solo this time was leagues better.

When it came time to vote, the whole club put their hands up for Ayaka's performance. She teared up a little, but only I saw her dab at her eyes. Everyone else was still facing the other way.

*

'Risa!'

After rehearsal, Ayaka called out to me as I was leaving the school grounds.

'I know how much you wanted that solo,' she said. 'Why did you ask Ms Hasegawa to redo the audition?'

She had a desperate look on her face, and at first I wasn't sure why. She'd won the right to play the solo. Why should she care what my motivations were?

But, of course, that was just who she was. That desperate look was concern for me.

'You heard me play today,' I said. 'That was the best I'm capable of. I'm not the right person to take that solo, and that's that.'

'So you asked for a do-over expecting to lose? You idiot!' She grabbed a handful of my shirt at the chest, starting to tear up. 'You're an idiot!' she shouted again.

'I know,' I said cheerfully. 'But you know what? For the first time ever, I'm glad to be an idiot. It feels way better to own it.'

After fourteen years of this 'living' business, I was finally starting to understand who I was.

Ayaka trembled, her eyes downcast. 'Risa . . .' she said.

'Good luck with the solo. And don't worry – I'll be outplaying you again by graduation.'

After all, this wasn't over yet. There could be other pieces with trumpet solos. And if there were, I was determined to win one fair and square.

'Bring it on!' Ayaka said.

We shook hands anyway. Ayaka's tears had been replaced by a glint in her eye that made it clear she wasn't planning to make it easy for me.

From now on, I thought, *we can be proper rivals.*

To give the gist of what happened afterwards:

I decided it was time for some self-improvement. I started giving my full attention to what was going on around me – including what the teacher was saying in class.

In brass band, I got serious about practice. I drilled the fundamentals over and over, and I listened closely to the other members, ready to swipe the best parts of their playing.

My parents noticed and approved of the motivation I now showed alongside my composure.

My friends said that I'd changed – and they liked the new me more. This praise felt much better than the kind I'd received when I was eating those caramels.

Ayaka and I were on friendlier terms, too. She came to me a lot to discuss part-leader business – how to teach the underclassmen, what to put in her practice plans, and so on. And since she took her responsibilities seriously, asking for my advice meant that she accepted me as an equal.

If you put in the effort, eventually someone notices. I'd never put enough effort into anything before to realize how true this was.

Today, I went to visit the shrine at dusk again – my first visit since buying those caramels. I was hoping for the chance to thank Kogetsu, but I couldn't find the way to the shopping street.

I wasn't surprised. I'd been expecting it, in a way. That shopping street, and the Amberglow Candy Store in particular . . . I knew, somehow, that they weren't the sort of places humans were meant to go. It was just that, on that fateful day, enough coincidences had aligned to open the door to that other world.

I placed the box of caramels – now with just one

caramel left – in front of the shrine, put my palms together and bowed my head. 'Please accept this as an offering,' I said. 'I don't need anyone to act as my surrogate anymore.'

Once I was finished, I turned on my heel and left.

I wondered if the coincidences would ever re-align in a way that would let me see Kogetsu again. Maybe what I'd experienced had been a special privilege only available to children.

Feeling in a strange way that he might be watching over me right then, I looked up at the orange-tinted sky.

*

As the girl looked up at the sky, for the briefest of moments their eyes met. But she gave no sign of seeing him, and left the shrine with a spring in her step.

Kogetsu descended from his vantage point on the roof to the ground – a rare concession to real-ity, for him.

'She came nearer to the truth than any other

customer to date,' he mused. 'A fine reminder not to underestimate the young.'

He picked up the box she had left as an offering and smiled, his eyes narrowing.

'But she was still mistaken about one thing. The truth is, she *was* being tormented by a spirit of ill fortune when she met me. She seemed to have attracted it by attributing the negative consequences of her own actions to "bad luck" . . .'

Kogetsu removed the last caramel from its box and gazed into space.

'But that spirit has departed. How fortunate for her. Now to take my sample . . .'

Sitting on his palm, the caramel was enveloped in amber. He returned the now-empty box to its place outside the shrine, and vanished.

CHAPTER 5

Enlightening Candy Apples

'Waaah! Waaah!'

The wails filled our apartment. Our baby was bawling and flailing her limbs, desperate to get through to me.

'All right, all right!' I said. 'I'm coming!'

I had no reason to think anything was seriously wrong, but Sakura's crying still made me nervous. What would the neighbours think if they heard?

When feeding her stopped the crying right away, all was well. But when it didn't, I felt so helpless that I wanted to cry myself.

As much as I adored her, spending all day alone with Sakura felt like being sealed away from the rest of society in a tiny, isolated world.

I was almost thirty. I'd fallen pregnant right after marrying my husband, and then left my job to be a full-time homemaker. I'd considered taking maternity leave instead of quitting entirely, but my husband wanted me to focus on Sakura during her early years, at least.

Our parents all lived too far away to help with everyday tasks, so the only person I could rely on was my husband. But ever since Sakura's birth he'd been distant with me.

He never got up to check on Sakura when she cried at night. At best, he stirred just enough to pointedly mumble 'The baby's crying' in an irritable, sleepy voice. He never apologized for leaving all the chores to me, or thanked me for my contribution to the household.

Leaving my job did free up time to spend with Sakura, but there was still as much to do around the house as before. To be honest, life was much easier back when all I had to do was juggle the housework with a regular job. Having that connection to the rest of society had also made me feel more secure, and back then my husband even offered the occasional word of gratitude or appreciation.

'Maybe his affections are fading,' I sighed.

Fatherhood makes some men more domestically

oriented, but others turn into workaholics, driven to earn more for their family. My husband was probably the latter. Or maybe he just wanted to avoid spending time with us.

'You're the only one who needs me, Sakura,' I said, looking down into the cot and prodding her cheek.

We named her after the cherry blossoms because she was born in the spring. My husband's name was Itsuki, meaning 'standing tree', and mine was Chika, 'a thousand flowers', so we wanted our daughter's name to share the same botanical theme.

Eight months had passed since that joyful spring day. Winter was well and truly here.

I couldn't even remember doing anything but parenting over the past eight months. I hadn't been to the hair salon in forever, or met up with my friends. It was no exaggeration to say that my every waking hour was devoted to Sakura.

That evening, I put Sakura in her pushchair and went to the supermarket. The weather was nice, and Sakura was in a good mood, so I decided to turn the journey home into a walk by taking a more roundabout route.

We'd moved to this town after getting married, so apart from the major landmarks I actually didn't know it very well. The other side of the main road was uncharted territory to me.

As I trundled the pushchair down a street I seldom visited, I noticed a small shrine standing at the top of a staircase up a little hill.

The shrine was surrounded by tall trees, which, combined with the elevation from street level, heightened the feel of a sacred space, sealed off from the rest of the world. That kind of refuge was exactly what my weary soul needed right now.

There was a ramp beside the steps that looked wide enough for the pushchair. Maybe a quick break was in order.

But when I reached the top and entered the shrine precinct, I saw that there was nothing there but the main building – no benches, for example. It clearly wasn't designed to be a place one sat in quiet contemplation.

Sakura had been gleefully active while we shopped, kicking and throwing her arms around, but she was sound asleep in her pushchair now, and I was hoping I would be able to relax a little here, too. Disappointed as I was, I decided to pray at the shrine before leaving.

Quietly and carefully, so as not to wake Sakura, I put my coins in the offering box and rang the bell. I prayed for the safety and well-being of our family, but then had the nagging feeling that my true desires lay elsewhere.

A chill ran down my back. I shivered and zipped up my down coat, preparing to leave. But then I was struck by the odd sense that something was amiss, and turned back for another look.

There was something about the scenery that didn't sit right. But what was it?

'Aha!'

There was an opening in the trees around the shrine. A single, narrow gap that looked purposefully made.

When I went over to examine it more closely, I realized that beyond the gap was a long, straight road that led to a quaint-looking shopping street.

This was a surprise to me. I did all my shopping at the supermarket, and hadn't even realized there were other options. But I decided to check it out – maybe they'd have better prices here.

As I made my way down the street, the un-surfaced road made the pushchair rattle, but Sakura didn't stir. Perhaps the vibrations were soothing.

Now that I was further along the shopping street, I noticed a few strange details that hadn't been obvious from the outside. Instead of streetlights, it was strung with lanterns, and some of the signs weren't in Japanese. Also, virtually all the stores I'd passed so far were closed.

'I think this was a mistake,' I sighed, and decided to turn back at a convenient point.

Just then, my eyes met those of a little girl peeking at me from behind a store. She looked a little too young for school. Her black hair was in an old-fashioned bowl cut, and she was wearing a red kimono, of all things. At another time of year, I might have guessed she was dressed for a Shichi-Go-San shrine visit with her parents, but the season was wrong for that. Maybe she had some other family observance today.

'Well, aren't you lovely!' I said. 'Hello!'

She approached me cautiously. I gave her a smile, which seemed to put her at ease. She peered into the pushchair.

'Have you seen many babies before?' I asked.

She thought briefly, then nodded.

'Do you like little children?'

Another yes. Maybe she had a younger sister or brother.

Her silent replies and blank look were a little concerning, but maybe she was wary of talking to strangers.

I smiled as I watched the girl gaze at Sakura's sleeping face – and then I noticed something strange.

'Hm?'

There seemed to be two lumps appearing on her head. They were growing bigger even as I stared. I rubbed my eyes.

'Is your head all right?' I asked her. 'Did you bump it on something?'

Her hands flew up to cover the bumps, but it was too late: two ears that looked just like a tanuki's popped out between her fingers.

The girl scampered off as I stared in shock. And when she turned her back to me, I saw what seemed to be a round, bushy tail, holding up the hem of her kimono . . .

'I must be more tired than I thought,' I muttered.

I was having blurry vision lately. I'd probably just mistaken some regular bumps for ears. As for that thing that looked like a tail, weren't fake tails all the rage not so long ago? I was sure they still sold them at theme parks.

Once I got home, I decided, I'd have a quick lie-down before making dinner. If I pushed myself too far and collapsed, there was a lot of parenting and housework that wouldn't get done at all.

I didn't run into anyone else as I walked on to the T-junction at the end of the shopping street, which was smaller than I'd realized. But at the very end of the street was one shop that did stand out from the others. Its sign read AMBERGLOW CANDY STORE. I didn't know what the 'Amberglow' part meant, but at least it sounded cosy.

The building looked as old as the others, but much better maintained. It was practically glowing in the light of the pink lantern outside.

I wondered if they sold anything Sakura could eat. I tried to give her healthy snacks, like dried sweet-potato strips and additive-free *tamago boro*, instead of junk food. A specialist store like this, I thought, might have some hand-made sweets she could enjoy as well.

One hand on the pushchair, I opened the weighty door with the other. The dim interior came into view.

It wasn't exactly roomy, but the spaces between the display shelves were generous enough and there were no other customers inside, so it didn't seem like the pushchair would get in the way.

'Welcome.'

The greeting came just as I managed to get my pushchair up the step inside the entrance.

'Oh, hello –' I began, turning towards the direction the voice had come from. But I froze before I could finish my sentence. The young man standing there was absolutely stunning.

Elegant, sculpted features; silky golden hair; and, for some reason, wearing *hakama* trousers. At first it struck me as unusual to see such a bright hair colour with traditional Japanese clothes, but he wore the look with such nonchalance that I wondered if it was actually in these days.

He glanced at the pushchair and flashed a smile.

'This is unexpected,' he said. 'I don't believe we've ever been visited by two customers together before.'

'Two . . . ?' I repeated, puzzled, then realized that he was counting Sakura, too. That was nice of him. But could he really mean that every single customer so far had come alone?

'I am Kogetsu, the proprietor, and this is the Amberglow Candy Store on Gloaming Lane. Please take all the time you need to browse.'

The shopping street was called 'Gloaming Lane'?

'Th-thank you.'

I strolled around the shop, taking it all in. It had a lot of traditional-looking *wagashi* for a place that called itself a candy store. But there were also more casual snacks on offer, like *konpeito* and caramels.

Then my eye landed on the biggest, reddest confection of all.

'A candy apple . . . ?'

It was the kind people sold from stalls at festivals: a whole apple, jabbed through with a disposable wooden chopstick and coated in hard red candy. There was only one on the shelf. It was a good size smaller than the apples they sold at the supermarket – some kind of miniature variety, maybe?

'I see the candy apple has caught your interest.'

Kogetsu's voice came from behind me, making

me jump. I must have been so lost in my thoughts that I hadn't noticed him approaching.

'Yes,' I said, flustered. 'I thought they only sold those at festivals, so I was surprised to see one on the shelf.'

'They happen to be a personal favourite of mine. I particularly appreciate the way the translucent coating, unlike other forms of candy, reveals what lies within. Don't you wish the same were true of the human heart?'

His golden eyes bored into my soul. I felt my heart beat faster.

I'd often wished I could see into my family members' hearts. Sakura couldn't speak yet, and sometimes my husband refused to. If I could see for myself what made her grizzle and what prompted my husband's irritable moods, maybe we'd be able to communicate better.

Also, while I wasn't necessarily sold by Kogetsu's sales pitch, the thought of biting into a candy apple did hold some nostalgic appeal. I hadn't had one since I was a little girl.

'Do you have another one of these?' I asked.

The candy apple was too big for Sakura, but only

buying one seemed a bit impolite. The extra one could be for my husband.

'I believe we do, in fact,' said Kogetsu. 'I shall check the storeroom. Please wait here.'

He went back behind the counter at the rear of the store and pulled open a sliding door. In the room beyond, I saw an open cabinet almost as high as the ceiling, with shelves like a bookcase completely packed with what appeared to be glass jars. It didn't look like the sort of thing a candy store would have out back.

Sensing my gaze, Kogetsu turned to me with narrowed eyes.

'No peeking, please.'

His expression was mild, but his eyes were unsmiling. Was he angry with me? I shivered and felt goosebumps rise on my arms.

'I – I'm sorry,' I said meekly, although I didn't think I'd done anything to make him *that* upset.

Kogetsu put his index finger to his lips, as if sharing a secret, and said, 'Curiosity killed the cat. Better to forget what you have seen here.'

'O-of course,' I agreed.

Maybe he just didn't want me to see how messy it was back there.

He soon returned with another candy apple, and rang up both of them for me at the register. They were much cheaper than festival prices.

'Thank you very much,' he said. 'And please be sure to observe the usage and dosage regulations.'

*

Once I got home and put the groceries away, I lay down on the sofa, staring into space the whole time.

Well, that *was a strange place . . .*

From Kogetsu, the otherworldly proprietor, to the crumbling shopping street and little girl in a kimono, it had been like walking onto a movie set – and a well-made one, at that. I couldn't really remember going back to the shrine, or the walk back to our apartment. Had I really been that rattled? Because of one brief scolding by a good-looking man? As a woman of near thirty – and a *married* woman, at that – I was a little embarrassed.

I hugged a sofa cushion to my chest and sighed, and a notification arrived on my phone. It was my husband, letting me know he'd be home late. Still plenty of time left before dinner, then.

'Maybe I'll try that candy apple,' I said.

Sakura was engrossed in an anime DVD, but even if she happened to notice I was eating the candy apple, I had other snacks I could give her instead.

I removed the plastic wrapping and gave the candy-covered apple an experimental lick.

The coating tasted like the *bekko-ame* I'd eaten as a child – plain hard candy, in other words. Which made sense. You could only do so much with melted sugar and red food colouring.

Simple as it was, though, it was absolutely delicious. I'd always assumed it was the festival setting that made candy apples taste so good, but I was enjoying this one just fine in the comfort of my apartment. Perhaps it was the memories of my childhood home and times long past it evoked.

I took a bite from an area where the candy coating was thin, enjoying the crunchy texture. Tart apple juice filled my mouth, blending marvellously with the sweet candy.

'Yum,' I said.

A few bites were enough to sweep my fatigue away. If snacks were that effective at re-energizing you, maybe I should stop avoiding them. At least for those tough early years of parenthood.

'Sakura,' I called, glancing over to where she was watching her anime.

But what I saw made me doubt my own eyes.

'What . . . *is* that . . . ?'

Her body was surrounded by glowing red light. Or . . . was she actually the *source* of the glow?

'S-Sakura! Are you all right?!'

I rushed across the room and picked her up. She looked at me, puzzled.

The red light was like an aura, snugly enveloping her silhouette. It didn't feel hot – it didn't feel like anything, in fact. Sakura looked unconcerned, and I didn't see any obvious ill effects.

Was something wrong with my eyes? I'd never heard of hallucinating glowing auras as a symptom of eye trouble, but given that floaters existed, surely a condition that tinted part of your field of vision red wasn't outside the realm of possibility.

Experimentally, I closed my left eye, then my right. It didn't make a difference. Even when I shifted my gaze, the red glow only appeared around Sakura.

'Well, that's just great . . .'

Our regular eye doctor wasn't open this late, so I'd have to wait until tomorrow morning. With luck, of course, the problem would resolve itself before then.

Seeing a doctor about my own health issues was always a trial, because Sakura had to come along, too. I knew this was no time to complain about that, but still . . .

I remembered an older colleague at work telling me about life after thirty. Fatigue got harder to resolve, she said, and all sorts of minor aches, pains and other issues started to appear. At the time I'd brushed off her warnings, saying that it probably depended on the person. I definitely hadn't imagined this happening to me.

Ignoring the red glow, I fed Sakura and put her to bed. Eventually I heard the door open and my husband's weary, 'I'm home.'

'Welcome home,' I said as I walked to our entranceway. 'You must be – exhausted . . . ?'

The last word came out as a hoarse whisper. My eyes flew open in shock and I stood rooted to the spot.

There was my husband, sitting down facing the door, removing his shoes with a sigh. And from his back radiated a faint red glow.

'But . . . why . . . ?'

The light of his aura was weaker than Sakura's. For the first time, I realized that the translucent red was like a candy apple's coating – and that all this had started right after my first bite of the candy apple I had bought from Kogetsu.

I thought back on my eerie experiences in Gloaming Lane and the Amberglow Candy Store. Could that candy apple be making me hallucinate? But that was ridiculous.

'Chika? Everything okay?'

I'd been frozen and silent for so long that my husband was starting to look worried.

'Y-yep! Everything's fine!'

If it really was some kind of condition, I'd have to discuss it with him. But for some reason, instinct told me to hide it.

'Do you want to take a bath before dinner?' I asked, so as not to leave an opening for more questions from him. 'Oh – we're having cream stew today.' Cream stew was one of his favourite dishes.

'Really? Maybe I'll eat dinner first,' my husband said, breaking into a radiant smile.

And, as he did, the red light around him flared up. I cried out in surprise.

My husband was alarmed by this outburst, but I was too shocked to speak. Eventually, in a testy tone of voice, he said, 'What? Why do you keep staring at me?'

'I-I'm sorry,' I said. 'I'll go warm up the stew.'

He grunted in acknowledgment. 'Let me just change out of this suit,' he said, and trudged towards the bedroom scratching his head. His aura had subsided again.

If I was seeing these auras because of the candy apple, then why did Sakura's and my husband's look so different?

My husband ate his cream stew with gusto. By the time he was finished, his aura was bright again, and it stayed that way until he went to bed. But when he woke the next morning, it was back to its initial faintness.

After my husband left for work, I decided to take Sakura out instead of visiting the doctor. We went to the park, where I ran into one of my mum friends who lived in the same apartment building. She had an aura, too, but it was even fainter than my husband's. Looking around the park, I noticed that everyone I knew personally had similarly faint auras, while those I'd never spoken to had none at all.

So, not everyone had an aura – only the people I knew. And the strength of the aura varied. To indicate . . . what?

By then, of course, I was sure this wasn't an eye condition. For better or worse, that candy apple had caused it. I decided to keep the other one, meant for my husband, hidden in the cupboard for now.

I particularly appreciate the way the translucent coating, unlike other forms of candy, reveals what lies within. Don't you wish the same were true of the human heart?

Kogetsu's comment had to be some kind of hint.

Observing Sakura closely over the course of the day, I noticed that when she was hungry, or wanted to be held, her aura grew brighter. But when I scolded her or things didn't go the way she wanted, it got fainter again.

Noticing the way her aura flared particularly strongly when she wanted my attention, I began to suspect that the red glow was an indicator of her affection towards me. That would explain why different auras glowed in different ways, and why only people who knew me had an aura at all.

It would also mean that my husband's affection for me was about one-third as strong as Sakura's. This was something I would have preferred not to have learned, even if I did know that a child's love for their mother was uniquely powerful.

When my husband came home that evening, unusually early for him, he had a cheerful smile on his face and strands of brown hair on his coat sleeves.

'Is this animal fur?' I asked, brushing it off his sleeves to flutter to the floor of our entryway. 'How did this get on you?'

'I petted a dog on the way home. Found him walking around at night all by himself.'

My husband loved animals, especially dogs. His dream was to buy a house with a yard big enough for a pet dog.

'Without its owner?' I said. 'Was it a stray?'

This was an alarming thought – you never knew what diseases a stray could carry.

'No, it seemed too comfortable around people to be a stray. Smooth, glossy fur, too. It was dark, so I couldn't see if it had a collar, but it was about as big as a Shiba Inu, I guess . . .'

'A Shiba . . . ?'

I plucked one of the remaining strands of fur from my husband's sleeve and held it up to the light.

It was pale brown in colour, and longer than you'd expect from a short-haired breed like a Shiba. In fact, it looked almost like fur from a –

'What's up with you lately?' my husband asked, interrupting my reverie. 'You zoned out when I came home yesterday, too.'

'Nothing's up,' I said. 'I was just wishing I could have petted it, too.'

'If its owner lives nearby, we might run into it again,' my husband said cheerfully.

I had to be overthinking things. We lived in an urban area – how could my husband possibly have run into a fox? I was probably still just shaken by that little girl on Gloaming Lane, who seemed to have a tanuki's ears and tail.

Come to think of it, Kogetsu's long, narrow golden eyes and sharp profile were a little fox-like, too . . . and he did sell things with mysterious powers. Would it be so odd if he was a fox?

But if that was true, then I'd taken Sakura to a hidden lane where young tanuki roamed the streets, and bought candy apples from a man who was actually a fox in disguise. Just imagining it sent a chill down my spine.

'No,' I said, hugging myself. 'There's no way.'

I'd never been able to handle tales of *yokai* and ghosts and the like. I decided not to think about it anymore.

And in any case, buying mysterious candy from a handsome man who seemed to have strange powers sounded less like a ghost story and more like a fairy tale.

Once I understood that the red auras indicated affection, I started observing my husband more closely. My first takeaway was that affection levels were variable.

When he came home exhausted on weekdays, his aura was faint. On weekends, it got brighter. It also got brighter when I cooked something he liked for dinner, or made a special effort to be nice to him.

Presumably, this meant that workdays left him with no energy to spare for me, but once he got some rest on the weekend he was able to give me more of his attention. And it was obvious enough why a person would feel more affectionate towards someone who did nice things for them.

My husband's affections hadn't faded – at least, not in the way I'd imagined it. Like everyone else, he just got stretched too thin sometimes. He was still struggling to adjust to life with Sakura as part of our family unit, similarly to the way I felt over-whelmed caring for her sometimes.

If affection levels were variable, then I could increase his by changing how I acted. All it would take was more devotion.

And so, wanting to see my husband glow more brightly, I redoubled my efforts to keep on top of the housework. When my husband came home, I strove to be a pleasant and stimulating conver-sationalist, and on days off, even when we took Sakura to the shopping mall, I made sure my hus-band had some alone time. On the nights he went out drinking and didn't come home until after midnight, I met him at the door with a smile – and no complaints.

In time, my husband's aura was as bright as Sakura's.

If only I could see their hearts, I'm sure we'd be able to communicate better. My wish had been granted – so why did I still have this nagging feeling inside?

Was I really satisfied with this outcome? What if my real wish was something else entirely?

I remembered making my wish at the shrine, and realizing that it wasn't what I truly wanted.

What *did* I want, then? My husband was kinder to me now, his affection for me was deeper – surely that should have satisfied me.

On Sunday evening, I was preparing dinner while my husband played with Sakura in the living room. He was actually better at this than me, and judging by her delighted squeals, she was having the time of her life.

'Chika!' my husband called as I was chopping a spring onion. 'Can I eat this?'

'Hmm?' I said absently. 'Eat what?'

Once I was finished with the onion, I leaned forward and peered through the kitchen's open passageway into the living room.

My husband was biting into the second candy apple.

'No!' I cried.

Why? How? I'd made sure to hide it in a cupboard he never opened!

I ran over to stop him, but it was too late. He was already chewing, and there was a big, clear bite taken out of the candy apple in his hand.

I sank to the living-room floor, defeated.

'Oh, sorry,' he said, turning to face me. 'Was this – *whoa!*' He covered his eyes and recoiled in shock.

My secret was out. Now my husband could see how much affection people felt for him, too.

And I'd been saving the extra candy apple for myself, for when the original one wore off . . .

I hung my head, devastated, but my husband's reaction to this development wasn't what I expected.

'Wh-what's going on?' he shouted in a panicky voice, waving his hands in front of his eyes. 'I've gone blind! All I can see is this dazzling red light!'

'Huh?' I said, looking up. So . . . for him the light wasn't just auras around people?

Confused, I moved in closer, making him jump and cover his eyes again.

'It just got even brighter!'

A suspicion entered my head. 'Stay right there!' I said, standing up. 'Don't move!' I retreated to the far end of the living room, as far from my husband as I could get. 'How's this? Uncover your eyes and check.'

My husband cautiously moved his hands, then said, 'It worked. The light's gone down enough to see what's around me now.' He looked relieved. 'But where are you, Chika?'

'Over here, by the door.'

He squinted, trying to see me, then blinked in surprise.

'Wait . . . Are *you* the one glowing?! You're so bright, I can't even see you!'

'Yes,' I said. 'It's me.'

I felt like bursting into tears. If I was bright enough to dazzle him, what did that say about my affection levels? I loved him much, much more than even an infant loves its mother.

'I'm sorry,' I said. 'This is all my fault.'

'What are you talking about?' my husband said, furrowing his brow.

Sakura's mouth hung open as she looked back and forth between our serious expressions, still holding her doll.

I had my husband put on some sunglasses, and then told him about the candy apples. The whole story, from the moment Sakura and I stepped into that mysterious shopping street.

Once I was finished, my husband looked at Sakura, who was sitting on the carpet watching a children's television show we'd recorded. 'I see,' he said. 'You're right – Sakura's glowing, too. I just didn't notice at first because your aura was so dazzling.'

My husband accepted the peculiar tale without question, presumably because he'd experienced the effect of the candy apple for himself.

'So the stronger someone's affection is towards you, the brighter their aura is?' he asked.

'Right,' I said.

'How bright did mine look to you?'

I hesitated, but answered honestly. 'Right now it's about as bright as Sakura's. But it was fainter before.'

'Oh.' He sighed. 'Meanwhile, you care for me so much that I can't even look at you without shades?'

After another long pause, I said, 'Yes.' As I spoke the word, I realized what my true wish was. It wasn't just for us all to be safe and happy, or to know how my husband felt – it was for him to understand how much *I* cared for *him*.

At last, I understood what that nagging feeling meant – but who would have imagined I'd find out this way?

'Which explains why you've been doing so much for me lately,' my husband said. 'I'm sorry I didn't realize how much you love me. And I'm sorry I've left all the parenting and housework to you, too.'

He lowered his head in apology, then scratched his chin in embarrassment.

'To be honest, though, I'm happy to hear it. After Sakura was born, all your attention was directed at her, right? I thought the feelings you had when we first started dating were gone forever.'

Was that why he'd thrown himself into his work? Because I'd been so busy with Sakura that I'd had no time for him, and he felt there was no place for him at home?

The reason his light was shining more brightly was because I'd started talking to him more.

In retrospect, after Sakura was born, we'd had much less time for conversations as a couple. And it was me, not him, who had been the first to respond snappishly to his attempts at initiating them. When he'd tried to talk to me while Sakura was grizzling, for example, I probably hadn't bothered to hide my irritation.

I'd been critical of him, but I hadn't reflected on my own behaviour.

'You don't mind that I'm this bright? It's not . . . clingy?'

Imagine having to deal with a wife who gets so worked up about these things that she went out and bought these weird candy apples, I thought.

'Are you kidding?' he said. 'Who wouldn't want their wife to like them?'

I'd asked the question tearfully, but he responded with genuine laughter.

'From now on, I'll make sure to show you how I feel,' he continued. 'And I'll do more of the parenting and housework. So if you ever feel unappreciated or uncertain, you just tell me.'

'Okay!'

I hadn't expected to ever hear anything like that from him. My vision blurred as my eyes brimmed with tears.

'I love you, Chika,' he said.

'I love you, too.'

He wrapped his arms around me, and I started sobbing into his chest. I hadn't cried like this since I was a child.

And then, feeling better, I looked up at him and saw that the red light had disappeared.

'Your aura is gone,' I said, puzzled.

My husband removed his sunglasses. 'Huh,' he said. 'Yours, too.'

We exchanged a smile. How long had it been since we'd said 'I love you' to one another, or held each other like this? And it was all thanks to those candy apples.

'Maybe that Kogetsu character was the kami of matrimonial bliss,' my husband said. Clearly, he'd been thinking along the same lines as me.

'Could be,' I said.

'Do you think I could visit that store? I'd like to thank him.'

'Me too. But I don't think we can get there anymore.'

In fact, somehow I was sure of it – and our auras vanishing felt like confirmation that we didn't need to go back anyway.

Before, I hadn't seen either of us clearly. But now my vision was unclouded, and I got the feeling that people like that didn't need the Amberglow Candy Store anymore. And, no doubt, we were happier for it.

'If that's what you think, then that's probably how it is,' my husband said.

'Thank you for believing me.'

We hugged again – but this time, Sakura, who was tired of watching television, tried to wedge herself between us.

'Sakura!' I said, exasperated.

'No problem,' my husband said. 'I can hug you both at once. Watch this!'

Sakura squealed with glee. The three of us laughed together as the evening light flooded through the living-room window.

From now on, I decided, *I'll convey my love to my husband with words. And when I want his affection, I'll let him know, too.*

Even tiny Sakura knew how to express her need for love and reassurance. I could stand to learn a lot more from her.

*

In the sprawling parking lot beside the apartment building stood a tall poplar tree. Atop the tree was a familiar silhouette, with fox ears and *hakama* trousers.

'Chika's field of view was so constricted when she visited the store, she noticed neither the days it was closed nor the names of the products. Now, however, she seems to have recovered her innate powers of observation.'

As Kogetsu kept watch through the lace curtain across one of the apartment windows, three shadows came together. His eyes narrowed.

'Rescuing that candy apple from the cupboard and placing it on the table to be found may have been meddlesome,' he murmured, his tail swishing back and forth. 'But I could not resist doing a kindness to someone so favourably disposed to animals. Even if, truth be told, I do not much enjoy being petted.'

Kogetsu crooked a finger. The second candy apple materialized half-eaten in his hand.

'Another sample obtained,' he said. 'I know nothing of families, but I suppose they must have something special to offer if they make Chika so happy.'

He peered at the apartment window, his eyes narrowing again. In his hand, the candy apple was soon encased in amber.

And then Kogetsu was gone, leaving only the strange impression that he had wished to linger yet.

Valedictory Mame Daifuku

Kogetsu lay in his bedroom, gazing up through his window. It was the night of the new moon, and a darkness deeper than usual spread across the sky.

'I always remember him on nights like this,' he murmured.

Kogetsu crawled out of his futon, pulled a haori jacket over his shoulders, and positioned himself in the window alcove, his back braced against the frame. It was cold outside, and his exhalations fogged the glass as he studied the sky.

'How many decades ago was it now? A century, perhaps? The flow of human time is so elusive.'

This is a story from before Kogetsu opened the Amberglow Candy Store.

In those days, Western culture was just taking

root in this country. The streets were filled with life and the people threw themselves into every new fad with wild abandon, but kimono were still more common as everyday garb than Western clothes. Such was the age in which our story takes place.

*

It began with simple thoughtlessness. Kogetsu hadn't been hungry, or even especially set on eating the confection in question.

The *nerikiri* camellia placed as an offering at the shrine had caught Kogetsu's eye, that was all. But when he picked it up without concealing himself from human eyes –

'Stop, thief!'

At this cry from behind him, Kogetsu slowly turned around. A young man with virile features was stomping towards him. He was about as tall as Kogetsu, but his muscular build made him seem larger. He wore a kimono and haori in subdued colours.

'That was given as an offering to the kami!' the man shouted.

When he got a better look at Kogetsu, his eyes widened briefly. He looked closely at Kogetsu's hair.

'Is that hair real?' he asked. 'Can you speak Japanese?'

'I can, yes,' said Kogetsu. 'What of it?'

Put on the receiving end of the questioning, the man shook his head hurriedly. 'Sorry,' he said. 'I didn't realize you were from overseas, since you're wearing those *hakama* and all. Must be hard to find work in these parts.'

Kogetsu hesitated, unsure where this was leading, then offered a non-committal 'Indeed.'

'I knew it,' the man said. 'You were hungry. Listen – you can't have anything I've already offered to the kami, but you're welcome to these instead.'

He opened a furoshiki he was holding to reveal an assortment of confections, each one small enough to fit on the palm of a hand.

A beat too late, Kogetsu realized that the man had mistaken him for an out-of-work foreigner, and was essentially offering him alms.

Kogetsu could have refused, but that would have required tiresome effort. Besides, the man was already explaining the bag's contents to him: 'This one is called *yokan*. Now, this one . . .'

Very well, then. It was unlikely that Kogetsu would meet this human again. He had no particular interest in humanity and no intention of becoming involved with any of them, so he decided to let the conversation run its course.

'Are there any of these you can't eat?' the man asked.

'I've never tried any, so I couldn't say.'

'Right, right,' the man said. 'In that case, take them all.'

He cheerfully handed Kogetsu the whole furoshiki. It wasn't heavy, but Kogetsu found it unpleasant to suddenly have both hands full.

'What's your name?' the man asked.

'Kogetsu.'

'"Kogetsu"'. Well, that sounds Japanese enough. I'm Akifumi Kohaku,' the man said, not waiting for Kogetsu to ask. 'You know the Kohakuya, that confectionery on the main street over there? That's my family's place.'

'"Akifumi",' Kogetsu repeated. 'Of the Kohakuya.'

Akifumi's broad-shouldered physique seemed

more appropriate to some kind of soldier or patrol-man. Was the work of a confectioner so gruelling? If so, there was no sign of it in the delicate sweets themselves.

'Where do you live, Kogetsu?'

'That way,' Kogetsu said, pointing towards the back of the shrine. It wasn't a lie. At the rear of the shrine precinct was the entrance to a road hidden from the eyes of normal humans. The Gloaming Lane shopping street – and, beyond it, Kogetsu's home.

'Nearer than I thought. That makes things easier!'

Akifumi clapped Kogetsu on the shoulder. Kogetsu jumped and stiffened, not used to being touched.

'Next time you've got an empty stomach and nothing to eat, drop by the store,' Akifumi said. 'If you'll settle for practice sweets, you can try some more things I've made.'

Beaming, Akifumi said his goodbyes and hur-ried off.

'It seems I have been drastically misunder-stood,' Kogetsu mused. 'Still, he seemed far from wicked, as humans go – albeit prone to leaping to conclusions.'

The conversation had been a short one, but Kogetsu felt utterly drained. He sighed. Dealing with energetic people always made him uncomfortable.

If he abandoned the sweets at the shrine, Akifumi would be bound to run across them again. Kogetsu saw no choice but to take them home with him.

In the darkening twilight, Kogetsu trod down Gloaming Lane. The street was lined on both sides with establishments of every kind, but there was no one else in sight, and very few *noren* curtains hung out to welcome potential customers. The residents here had no serious interest in doing business to begin with. Kogetsu had settled among them some time ago, and was still unable to decide how to support himself. But he could live without working, so his desire to do so was minimal. The same could have been said of all his fellow *ayakashi*, the creatures of folklore and mystery who had lived in secret alongside humanity since time immemorial.

But only outcasts among the *ayakashi* lived on Gloaming Lane, which lay on the outskirts of the Hidden Town, caught between the real world and the world of spirits. Some were simply eccentric, while others were *han-yo* like Kogetsu – half-*ayakashi* – whose powers were unstable. In any case, the lane was home to a motley crew of misfits who had been ostracized from the more central parts of town.

Since very few other *ayakashi* were inclined to visit such a place, customers were few and far between on Gloaming Lane. Lost and wandering humans found their way in occasionally, but none of the residents went out of their way to interact with them when they did.

Kogetsu sometimes visited the human world to while away the time, but he was in the minority. Most of the lane's residents never left its bounds.

'All I want is to loaf about, indifferent and indolent, with a way to stave off the tedium when it rears its head,' Kogetsu sighed. He had long since tired of life.

Reaching the T-junction at the end of the lane brought him face to face with the building he called home. It had originally been a store of some kind, but its proprietor had long since disappeared. Kogetsu had concluded that no one would care if he took up residence there, and so far he had been correct.

'If I had been born a human, my life would have run its course in the merest of instants. Why was it my fate to be born a *han-yo*?'

Because Kogetsu was half *ayakashi*, half human, neither the Hidden Town nor the human world truly felt like home to him. He was an outsider of no fixed abode, drifting with the current like a jellyfish.

By the time of his earliest childhood memories, he was already living alone. He did not even know his parents' faces. He assumed he had been abandoned, with neither parent willing to raise a *han-yo* child.

'That man I met today was exactly my opposite,' Kogetsu said. 'Humans like that are too busy pursuing dreams and goals to succumb to uncertainty or self-doubt. Fate would never bring them here.'

He glanced at the furoshiki, sitting where he had unceremoniously placed it in his bare, unfurnished bedroom. If he did not eat the sweets, they would remain there permanently, so he felt little choice but to begin.

The first confection he pulled out was a *nerikiri* camellia – a hand-sculpted marvel, much like the one he had picked up at the shrine. Had Akifumi made camellias because it was winter now? Kogetsu had not realized that sweets could express the changing seasons.

When he drew the camellia from its little box and held it between two fingers, he found it softer than expected. Any more pressure, and he might squash it flat.

'So finely made, yet so fragile. How troublesome.'

Kogetsu took a small, cautious bite. The refined sweetness of the azuki bean paste called *anko* filled his mouth.

'Very sweet,' he said. 'And yet . . .'

And yet he did not find the sweetness unpleasant. He ate the whole thing, and found himself hungry for more.

By the time he went to bed, Kogetsu had eaten the *nerikiri*, a piece of chestnut *yokan*, and a ball of mochi studded with sweet beans, called a *kanoko* or 'fawn' after its dappled appearance.

*

Some days later, Kogetsu was strolling down Gloaming Lane when he saw a figure looking around curiously with a furoshiki clutched to his chest. It was Akifumi.

'Kogetsu!' Akifumi said, raising a cheerful hand as he noticed Kogetsu, too. 'I was looking for you.'

Kogetsu was flabbergasted. 'What are you doing here?' he asked, hurrying towards him.

'Looking for you, that's what,' Akifumi said, apparently not noticing the look of horror on Kogetsu's face. 'You told me you lived behind the shrine, remember? Bit of a surprise, though – I didn't realize there was a shopping street back here. I saw *noren* with writing on them I can't read, and those red lanterns are out of the ordinary, too. Lot of foreigners living here, are there?'

'That's not – This place is –'

The Hidden Town was off-limits to normal humans. Only spectres, or people so troubled at heart that their very existence was cast into doubt, could even see the road that led here from the human world.

'This place is what?' asked Akifumi.

'. . . not the kind of place you should be,' Kogetsu said.

He had not taken Akifumi as someone beset by enough woe to destabilize his existence. Clearly, that was a mistake. He should never have told the man where he lived.

'You mean it's dangerous? Not to worry. I've got some muscle on me, even if I don't look it.'

'You *do* look it, as it happens.' If anything, Kogetsu found it more surprising that such a muscular man made such delicate confections. 'Please leave at once. Human visitors are a burden I do not need.'

If Akifumi stayed too long, he might meet one of Kogetsu's neighbours. There was little danger of that, as most kept to themselves inside their homes, but for word to get out that this was an *ayakashi* neighbourhood would be undesirable for many reasons.

But Kogetsu's shooing gestures only made Akifumi look sad.

'Pretty cold way to treat someone who came all this way to see you,' he said. 'And I brought sweets, too.'

'Sweets . . . ?'

Kogetsu's fox ears, currently invisible, twitched

at this. He had already eaten everything Akifumi had given him upon their meeting, and had been wistfully hoping for more – not that he would ever admit it.

'You ate that last batch, didn't you?' Akifumi said.

'Well, yes.'

'And they were good, weren't they?'

'Well . . . yes.' Kogetsu had to concede that point, too.

Akifumi grinned. 'Then you wouldn't mind if I dropped by your house for a visit, would you? Or begrudge me a cup of tea?'

'. . . I suppose I have no choice.'

Akifumi had got the better of him. But what else could Kogetsu do, with sweets on the line?

Kogetsu let Akifumi into his residence through the back entrance. The storefront took up so much of the building that his living quarters amounted to a single room, which had to serve as both parlour and bedroom.

'Pretty bare in here,' Akifumi said. 'No writing desk? No tea table?' There being no cushions, either, he sat himself down cross-legged on the tatami mat floor.

'I have no need for them,' said Kogetsu.

The room was eight tatami mats in size – just over a dozen square metres – and completely devoid of furniture. When it was time to sleep, Kogetsu would lay out some bedding he kept in the closet. He did not like having too many things in his living quarters. The accumulation of possessions felt constrictive and discomfiting to him.

Kogetsu placed a round wooden tray bearing a teapot and two cups directly on the tatami.

'You have a tea set, at least,' Akifumi said. 'That's a relief.'

'Even I drink tea,' Kogetsu said.

He poured green tea into both cups. He had never studied the approved procedure for brewing tea, instead simply using as many tea leaves as seemed appropriate. The result was always drinkable to him, so presumably Akifumi would find it tolerable, too.

'Good to hear it,' Akifumi said. '*Wagashi* go down better with tea. Speaking of which, look at my latest creation.'

Akifumi opened his furoshiki and carefully fished out a small white confection. It was plump and round, with ears, eyes and a mouth drawn on.

After a beat, Kogetsu said, 'And what is it? A rabbit?'

'A *snow* rabbit!' Akifumi said. 'You know, like kids make. Isn't it cute?'

Another beat. 'Indeed.'

'And it tastes as good as it looks. Try it.'

Akifumi went through every sample in the furoshiki, one by one, insisting that Kogetsu try all of them.

'I appreciate an audience with an appetite,' Akifumi said happily, slurping his tea.

Once all the sweets were gone and Kogetsu was sipping from his own cup, Akifumi leaned forward and asked, 'So, out of all the sweets you've tried so far, which was your favourite?' His eyes were sparkling, his expression full of life. The man truly loved his trade.

'Visually, the camellia or the rabbit, I suppose,' Kogetsu said. 'But in terms of taste and texture, I would have to say that one.'

He pointed at a little empty box that had once held a ball of *anko* densely studded with beans of various colours and sizes. It was not unlike the *kanoko* from the other day, but all the beans on that had been the same dark colour. This was presumably something different.

'The *mame kanoko*!' said Akifumi. 'Yeah, we use all kinds of beans for that one, not just azuki – gives it a fun texture, right?'

'Quite,' Kogetsu said.

The *mame kanoko* was also subtler in its sweetness. He could imagine eating one every day and never tiring of it.

'And don't think I didn't notice your weakness for cute presentation,' Akifumi said, clapping Kogetsu on the shoulder with a grin.

Kogetsu batted the hand away with a frown. 'Enough,' he said. 'If you insist on being overfamiliar, I will throw you out.'

'Aw, come on! No need to be embarrassed,' Akifumi said, ignoring the warning and putting his arm around Kogetsu's shoulders. 'Presentation is an important element for any confectionery!'

Was this man truly troubled at heart? Kogetsu could not see him as anything but a cheerful, confection-mad fool.

Perhaps he had somehow reached Gloaming Lane by mistake.

'All right, then. See you next time.'

Akifumi was finally preparing to leave. After the sweets were gone, he had continued to talk until nightfall, while Kogetsu listened and offered the occasional noncommittal response.

'Why did you come all this way today?' Kogetsu asked, as he saw him off at the back door. 'You had no way of finding my house, and there was no guarantee you would see me in the street.'

Despite himself, Kogetsu was genuinely curious. He supposed that spending most of the day with Akifumi was bound to spark some interest in him.

'Can't a man worry about his friend?' Akifumi asked.

'Friend? What friend?' Kogetsu frowned.

'You, of course! Who else would I be talking about?'

Kogetsu was stunned. After their single brief exchange on the shrine grounds, Akifumi considered him a friend? And a close enough friend to set out in search of with a furoshiki full of sweets?

As little as he knew about humans, even Kogetsu realized at that moment that Akifumi was kind-hearted to the point of naivety.

'What, you've never had a friend before?' Akifumi looked puzzled.

'No one I could call such, no.'

'Oh,' Akifumi said. 'Sounds like you've had it tough. But you'll be fine from now on. Whenever you need anything, just let me know.' With that, he put his hands on Kogetsu's shoulders and looked him square in the eye, a strange blend of sympathy and determination in his gaze.

Kogetsu sensed another misunderstanding afoot.

'I need nothing,' he said. 'Kindly refrain from visiting again.'

Then he closed the back door.

'There you go again!' Akifumi called through the door. He sounded cheerful as ever, with no sign of having taken offence. 'Too polite for your own good. I'll be back, don't you worry!'

Once Akifumi was gone, Kogetsu let out a deep sigh.

'What a tenacious fellow.'

He had no idea how to drive the man away.

But then again, perhaps he would not need to. Surely Akifumi would not visit again. A man so sure of himself finding his way here – it must have been some kind of error.

*

And yet Akifumi did return, again and again. He brought a fresh batch of *wagashi* each time, and shared more about himself with every visit:

'I'm the younger son down at the Kohakuya,' he explained. 'My older brother's going to take over the store, and I want to support him as an artisan.'

On another day: 'My father's been a confectioner for years and years. I need to catch up, so I put in some practice whenever I have a day off or a free moment after the store closes. That's where all these sweets come from – my practice sessions. Can't sell them in the store, so having someone to eat them is a huge help.'

On yet another day: 'The kami of that shrine can help merchants and traders prosper. Whenever

I make a decent batch of sweets, I leave one there as an offering.'

Eventually Kogetsu was quite the expert on Akifumi's domestic situation. And, he grudgingly conceded, he was learning a great deal from Akifumi's impromptu lectures on the sweets he brought.

After a certain point, trying to keep Akifumi at arm's length became more trouble than it was worth, and Kogetsu decided to let the man do as he wished. Presumably he would tire of their association once he found a sweetheart or some other diversion. A friendship this one-sided could not endure for long.

This gave Kogetsu an excuse for his inability to refuse Akifumi's visits, preserving his pride.

One day Akifumi said, 'You know, Kogetsu, you live on a shopping street – why don't you try opening a store? Your Japanese is good enough.'

Kogetsu was no longer surprised by Akifumi's familiarity by this point. 'That would be too much effort,' he said.

As far as Kogetsu was concerned, that was all the reason anyone needed. But Akifumi continued to press the matter.

'This building is mostly storefront. Only living in it is a waste. Isn't there anything you want to do with yourself? Any kind of trade you'd like to be in?'

'Hmm . . .' Kogetsu pretended to give the matter serious thought, but there was only one trade he was familiar enough with to suggest. 'If I were to open a store, I suppose it would be a confectionery.'

It was undeniable that tasting Akifumi's creations while listening to him explain them sparked a growing interest in *wagashi*.

But letting this information slip was his fatal mistake. And by the time he realized it, Akifumi was already beaming from ear to ear.

'A confectionery!' he cried, giving Kogetsu a hearty slap on the shoulder. 'Of course! In that case, I can help. Why didn't you say so sooner?!' Spit flew from his mouth in his excitement.

'I said *if* I were to open a store,' Kogetsu said. 'I have no wish to do so. Also, that hurts,' he added, smacking the back of Akifumi's hand.

As usual, Akifumi was undaunted. He wasn't even listening.

'If that's the plan, best to get started quickly.

Leave it to me! I'll head home to make all the preparations. See you on my next day off!'

'Preparations . . . ?'

But by the time Kogetsu had voiced his question, Akifumi was already racing out of his house.

Kogetsu shivered and pulled his haori tighter around him. 'I have an unpleasant feeling about this,' he said. And it seemed to him that, since meeting Akifumi, all of his worst premonitions had come to pass.

'So, Kogetsu, where's your kitchen?'

Several days later, Akifumi appeared at Kogetsu's door with a parcel dangling from each hand and an extra-large furoshiki-wrapped bundle. Kogetsu caught a glimpse of an iron pot lid inside, along with some kind of rod that was poking out as well.

'Quite a cargo,' Kogetsu said.

'Yep. All the tools of the trade. So, about this kitchen? – and don't try to tell me you don't have one!'

Kogetsu knew that if he *did* try to tell Akifumi that, the man would probably search the whole building until he found it for himself. Sighing and rubbing his forehead, he reluctantly led the way.

The kitchen took up a surprisingly large proportion of the building, and was equipped with a stove, sink and workbench. The former proprietor had presumably been in some kind of business involving kitchen work.

'This is nicer than I thought,' Akifumi said. 'Should do us just fine. I also brought some pre-made *anko* with me, just in case.' He patted the bundle on his back.

That must have been what was in the pot. But he would not need a whole pot just for Kogetsu. Which meant . . .

'What exactly are you planning to do today?' Kogetsu asked.

'Teach you how to make some *wagashi*.'

His worst premonition had come to pass. What a meddlesome pest Akifumi was!

'I don't recall asking you to do so.'

'But you did say you wanted to open a confectionery.'

'I said nothing of the sort!'

'No, no, I heard you very clearly.'

The argument went on for a while, but in the

end Kogetsu gave in. In truth, he had never stood a chance against a man so obliviously determined to help.

'Very well,' Kogetsu sighed. 'But if I prove not to be cut out for the work, I will give up on the spot.'

Having never prepared anything more complicated than tea, and certainly never cooked, Kogetsu found it difficult to believe he could make confectionery of any kind. It might have been faster simply to reveal his utter ineptness and wait for Akifumi to give up on him.

'Not to worry,' Akifumi said, supremely confident despite Kogetsu's own doubts. 'You'll be a natural at this – I can tell.'

'On what basis?'

'You like *wagashi*, don't you? That's the number-one requirement!'

Kogetsu found himself unable to respond. He had never been praised by anyone before, so perhaps he was simply off-balance.

But what was that warmth he had felt in his breath, for just a moment? A sense of growing excitement – the peculiar sensation of almost believing that even he could create something.

'This agitation is distracting,' he murmured, but by the time he was clutching at his chest through his haori, the sensation had already faded.

'Come on, what are you waiting for? Time to get ready!' Akifumi said. He deftly tied the loose sleeves of his kimono in place with a *tasuki* cord, then handed Kogetsu a spare cord and said, 'You too.'

Kogetsu copied Akifumi's example and secured his own sleeves.

'Pretty good! Now, wash your hands and let's get started. Today we're doing *ho-an*.'

Ho-an, Kogetsu knew from Akifumi's informal lecture series, was the art of wrapping an *anko* filling in an outer layer of something else. In this case, the 'something else' would presumably be the tinted *shiro-an*, *anko* made from white kidney beans instead of azuki beans, that filled the multi-layered box Akifumi had brought.

'*Ho-an* is a fundamental technique,' Akifumi continued. 'You need it for *nerikiri*, obviously, but also *manju*, *daifuku* – if you don't master *ho-an*, you won't get anywhere with any of them. Watch me do it and then give it a try.'

It seemed simple enough: roll *anko* into a ball,

and then wrap a thin circle of *shiro-an* around it so that it was evenly covered on all sides. But doing it well was surprisingly difficult. Each time Kogetsu thought he had succeeded, he would cut the result in half and see in cross-section that the *anko* and *shiro-an* had separated. Akifumi's sweets had no gap whatsoever at that border.

'It's the oil on your fingertips,' Akifumi told him. 'You have to do it faster, and touch the ingredients less. Like making nigiri sushi.'

Kogetsu knew nothing of sushi, but he recognized artisanal craft when he saw it. No doubt each kind of confection had its own tricks and techniques to learn – and Akifumi knew them all. For the first time, he felt respect for the man.

After wasting a few balls of *anko* on unsuccessful attempts, Kogetsu threw up his hands. 'Clearly you will not make an expert confectioner of me in one day,' he said. 'Shall we give up?'

'Who said anything about one day?' Akifumi replied. 'If anything, you're making more progress than I expected.'

'What?' The corners of Kogetsu's mouth twitched into a frown. 'What do you mean?'

'This is a long-term project!' Akifumi said. 'From now on, we practise on every day I have off. Evenings, too, when I'm free. Oh, and you don't have to worry about me – teaching you will help me improve, too.'

Kogetsu's face turned sour. 'You mean to occupy every one of my evenings from now on?'

'Not like you have anything else to do, is it?' Akifumi said, still beaming. 'Not to worry – put in the work, and you'll get the hang of it in no time.'

'And refusing would be a waste of breath, I presume.'

It was true that Kogetsu had nothing else to do. No acquaintances to visit, no goals to pursue. Not even the urge to ambush and toy with humans, the way some malicious *ayakashi* did. He spent his life whiling away the hours – what difference did it make if he did so by making sweets?

'Very well,' Kogetsu said. 'But I do have business of my own to attend to at times. When I tell you to stay away on a certain day, I must insist that you do so.'

The new and full moon. He absolutely could not meet Akifumi on those days. His powers grew unstable then, and he lost the ability to hide his ears and tail.

If Akifumi learned that Kogetsu was an *ayakashi*, it might serve to drive him away. But if word spread further than that, things could become troublesome. There had been humans, in the past, who had reviled *ayakashi* and sought to banish them. Dealing with such challenges would be exhausting.

'Of course!' Akifumi said. 'What kind of boor do you take me for?'

Half-surprised that Akifumi knew what a boor was, and half-exasperated by this new development, Kogetsu held his guest's gaze evenly.

From then on, Kogetsu spent almost every evening – and many days as well – on an intensive course of *wagashi* training.

After *ho-gan*, there was the shaping of *nerikiri* and the techniques for making *yokan*, *manju* and *monaka*. Akifumi seemed to have bought himself a spare set of tools, because he left a full set at Kogetsu's house.

Kogetsu was surprised to learn that the distinguished Kohakuya also sold less elegant treats, such as *konpeito*, *neriame* and caramels. This, Akifumi explained, ensured that the store always had something children could buy with their meagre pocket money, which seldom stretched to fine *wagashi*.

'They come in to buy caramels as kids, then grow up and start buying *wagashi*. That's what you call cultivating a customer base.'

And so Akifumi showed Kogetsu how to make these candies, too. Kogetsu was startled to learn that *konpeito* involved a two-week process.

Compared to *wagashi*, all of these candies were inelegant and overly sweet, but he had to admit that they were easy to snack on – and very small. They came in packs containing many, but those would empty out in no time.

Kogetsu was a quick learner, and before winter was out Akifumi was teaching him to make *anko* from scratch. Even Kogetsu had not realized how nimble his fingers were, or that he did not find absorbing, intricate work so distasteful.

One day, Akifumi turned up wearing a kimono the colour of pale matcha. A stray sakura petal was caught in his hair.

'Those sakura by the shrine are in full bloom,' he said. 'Want to go take a look?'

'Not especially,' Kogetsu said. 'They bloom every year.'

'Every year, sure – but you can only see it for a few days, remember? You can be so odd sometimes.'

Though Kogetsu looked to be in his mid-twenties, this was not his actual age. He had probably been born before Akifumi's great-grandfather was, and was not yet halfway through his expected lifespan. So it was no surprise that he took little interest in things that happened every year.

'In any case,' Akifumi said, frowning as he shaped some *nerikiri* into a cherry-blossom petal, 'if you're opening your own store, you'll be dealing with customers. You're polite and all, but that blank look of yours works against you. You seem a little . . . short on emotions, I guess.'

'Well observed,' Kogetsu replied. 'Emotions seldom trouble me, I find.'

'Oh, so you already knew? In that case, you can fix it.'

'I doubt it.'

Kogetsu didn't really understand emotions.

The way humans wept, raged and laughed their way through life was baffling to him. He could fake a smile, but had never felt anything strongly enough for his face to move of its own accord.

'Because you're not the sociable type, right? In that case, why not start with observing people instead?'

'Observing people . . . ? I'm not sure that will be much help.'

If observation were enough to enrich emotions, surely there would have been some change in him since meeting Akifumi.

'By the way,' Kogetsu said, 'do not come tomorrow. I will be otherwise engaged.'

Kogetsu felt his powers faltering as the new moon approached. But this growing instability was nothing compared to the nausea he felt on the night itself. As a newborn, he had reverted entirely to his fox form on those nights, vomiting and shivering until morning. He was able to handle himself a little better these days, but still spent the entire day in bed.

'You know,' Akifumi said slowly, 'not long ago, I thought back on the times you told me not to come.

I realized that it happens twice a month, and pretty regularly at that.'

Akifumi's hands fell still. He turned to look at Kogetsu.

Kogetsu also stopped working, and met Akifumi's gaze steadily.

I thought this man a harmless fool, but he is more perceptive than he seems . . .

'When I checked the calendar, I realized that all of those days were either a new or full moon. What 'business' are you taking care of, exactly?'

'I have no obligation to explain that to you.'

But Kogetsu's attempt at deflection proved fruitless. Akifumi's face started to harden.

'I've always thought it was strange,' he said. 'How does someone without a job keep himself fed?'

'What are you trying to say?' Kogetsu asked.

His kind had less need for food than humans, so they didn't need money to survive. If worse came to worst, he could simply transform into his fox form and hunt down a hare or bird.

'Well, you're a good-looking man. Pretty, even. You aren't selling *yourself*, are you? I've heard that the female body is influenced by the waxing and waning of the moon, so . . .'

Kogetsu snickered. 'Sex work?' He made a point of narrowing his eyes and smirking, and filled his voice with contempt. 'The idea makes my skin crawl. I don't even like *talking* to people, when I can help it.'

'Then why the new and full moon?' Akifumi asked.

Kogetsu was silent for a moment, then said, 'I dislike them. The new and full moon both. I do not wish to meet anyone on those days, or leave the house myself. There is nothing more to it.'

He removed his *tasuki* cord and slammed it onto the kitchen counter.

'Now, would you kindly leave for today?' he said.

Akifumi was obviously startled, but didn't try to argue. 'Sorry for prying,' he mumbled, and shuffled out of the house. With his drooping shoulders, he looked like a dejected dog.

Having spoken so harshly to him, Kogetsu was confident Akifumi had learned his lesson.

And yet . . .

*

The following evening, Kogetsu was lying in bed when he heard a hesitant knock on his bedroom window.

Kogetsu sat up. He knew at once who it was. Not that he had any other callers to begin with. Careful to stay where he could not be seen from the window – just in case – he called out, 'You again?'

'No need to open the window,' came the reply. It was Akifumi, as predicted. 'I expect you don't want anyone seeing you when you're feeling low.'

Kogetsu put a hand to his fox ears, which he was currently unable to hide. How had Akifumi known?

'I left some food by your back door. I know all you eat normally is *wagashi*, but I thought something more digestible might be better for you right now. There's *okayu*, and *amazake*, too – you'll want something sweet, right?'

He sounded genuinely concerned for Kogetsu's welfare.

'You really shouldn't have,' Kogetsu sighed. But the words were evidently too low to reach Akifumi's ears.

'I'll be off, then,' Akifumi called from outside. 'Make sure you get plenty of sleep after you eat.'

Kogetsu then heard the sound of someone running away in *zori* sandals.

Cautiously, he opened the back door. There at his feet was a furoshiki-wrapped bundle that radiated warmth. Inside it was a bento box full of rice porridge and a pot of *amazake*. Akifumi had even included a spoon.

Had Akifumi brought all this right after making it? On a dark, moonless night?

'Alas, my condition is not an illness,' Kogetsu muttered, 'so a change of diet will not help.'

Still, he felt guilty letting warm food cool. Sensing no other option, he tried a spoonful of *okayu*. The rice porridge was perfectly salted.

'What has he put in this?' Kogetsu said to himself. 'Turnips and – yomogi?'

The turnips lent the porridge a crispy texture, while the bitterness of the yomogi gave the flavour an intriguing twist. And wasn't it a medicinal herb, too? Had Akifumi taken even this into consideration?

By the time he'd finished the porridge, Kogetsu's belly was glowing with warmth.

'Mysterious,' he murmured. 'What I eat has no

connection to my powers, but I must admit I feel better, physically.'

Feeling sleepy after his warm meal, he drank just one cup of the *amazake* before returning to bed. He slept soundly until morning, without even the usual unpleasant dreams.

When Akifumi arrived the next day, he made no mention of the matter. Kogetsu followed suit, but the box, pot and spoon were all neatly washed and stacked. Out of the corner of his eye, he caught Akifumi checking that the containers were empty – and smiling to see that they were.

After that night, Akifumi came by and left some *okayu* for Kogetsu every new and full moon. He didn't call from outside anymore, though he stomped around so loudly that he woke Kogetsu every time. But Kogetsu didn't complain, because the *okayu* had a mysterious ability to make him feel better.

'Could there be something in food prepared by humans that makes it effective at stabilizing powers like mine . . . ? No, I've never heard anything like that. The yomogi, perhaps . . . ?'

The question so nagged at Kogetsu that on one occasion he experimentally picked the yomogi out and left it uneaten. But it made no difference to the *okayu*'s restorative powers. This discovery only deepened the mystery.

The first ominous shadow fell on their quietly established routine after spring gave way to summer and the evening cicadas began to call.

The Kohakuya was closed that day, so Akifumi had promised to come over for the afternoon. However, an unfamiliar youth with close-cropped hair arrived instead – and long after the appointed hour.

'Er – would you be Kogetsu, sir?' asked the youth.

'I am he,' Kogetsu said. 'And you are?'

'A messenger, sir, from Mister Akifumi,' the youth said. 'He injured his leg in an accident and can't walk right now. He won't be able to visit for a while.'

So this youth worked at Akifumi's household. Kogetsu had not realized that the Kohaku family was wealthy enough to have a staff, or that Akifumi was the kind of figure others referred to as 'Mister Akifumi'.

'I see,' Kogetsu said. 'Thank you for informing me.'

The youth accepted a tip for his trouble, bowed, and left. *He must also have some destabilizing anxieties,* Kogetsu mused, *or he would not have been able to find Gloaming Lane, even to deliver his message.*

You simply couldn't tell with humans – at least not from the outside.

'An accident?' Kogetsu murmured to himself. 'Evidently not life-threatening, so no intervention seems required . . . What to do, what to do?'

Having the day suddenly freed up like this left Kogetsu at a loss. He decided to visit the main thoroughfare in the human world – for no reason other than to kill time. It was his first such excursion in many months.

Emerging into the human world, he found its inhabitants dressed in light clothing that betokened summer. In centuries past this had been a castle town, and the main thoroughfare had been where merchants plied their trade outside the castle's fortified stone walls. The castle was gone now, but the neighbourhood was still a lively one, and Kogetsu heard animated conversation from every direction as the people strolled this way and that.

And somewhere on this street, apparently, was the Kohakuya. Kogetsu had never sought it out before, and was worried he would fail to identify it, but it was so large, with such a steady stream of customers, that it was easy to pick out among the other stores.

It was immediately clear that the Kohakuya was in a class of its own. The patina of age on the fine wooden sign conveyed a respectable gravity. Behind the storefront was a sprawling house and grounds that Akifumi presumably called home. The imposing double gates barring entry to these living quarters made it clear that uninvited callers were not welcome.

'Nor, however, do I wish to go to the trouble of arranging a formal visit,' Kogetsu murmured. He considered simply turning around and going home, but was reluctant to waste the effort he had made to come here. In the end he decided to enter, invisibly.

'Quite a respectable residence . . .'

The garden was large, with a pond full of koi. A gardener was trimming the pine trees as Kogetsu passed.

'I still struggle to reconcile it all. He doesn't *act* like a "Mister Akifumi" . . .'

But, on reflection, Akifumi's utter guilelessness, the way he drew closer to others without a second's hesitation, could have been derived from the kind of softness that came from living a sheltered life. Those who had grown up indulged tended to be indulgent with others, too. The exact opposite of Kogetsu.

'Now, then, which room is his?'

Revealing himself to Akifumi was obviously out of the question, but Kogetsu could at least see how he was doing.

Kogetsu walked around the house peering into each window one by one. Eventually he found Akifumi in a Western-style room with a wooden-framed bed. His heavily bandaged leg was in an elevated sling. The injury was clearly worse than Kogetsu had assumed. Akifumi's eyes were closed, but his brow was furrowed and his complexion pale.

Having never seen Akifumi in such a weakened state, Kogetsu took a moment to study him.

Then, to Kogetsu's shock, Akifumi's eyes opened.

'Kogetsu?' he said, looking towards the window.

Eyes still wide with surprise, Kogetsu rendered himself visible and opened the unlocked window.

'How did you know I was there?' he asked, climbing into the room. He didn't bother to remove his footwear, but Akifumi did not complain.

'Just a feeling I had. I wasn't expecting a visit from you.'

'I happened to be passing by,' Kogetsu said, averting his gaze. 'Nothing more.'

Akifumi smiled. 'Well, take a seat,' he said, gesturing at a chair and pulling himself into a sitting position.

'I heard you were in an accident,' Kogetsu said. 'May I inquire about the details?'

'Got hit by a horse-drawn carriage. Not run over, and my leg hardly hurts at all anymore, but I've been ordered to stay off it. I've been in more than a few dangerous situations lately, so my family's probably worried about me.'

'Dangerous situations? What do you mean?'

This was the first Kogetsu had heard of such a thing.

'Oh, you know. Close calls with horse-drawn carriages, like today. Almost falling over bridge railings, narrowly dodging iron pots falling from above. The usual.'

Kogetsu's concern that someone or something might have a grudge against Akifumi had clearly been wasted. The man was simply clumsy.

'Are you completely oblivious to the goings-on around you?'

'It's not like that,' Akifumi protested. 'It happens when I'm distracted – a carriage will happen to barrel my way just as the thong on my *geta* breaks, or I'll bump into someone and get knocked off-balance at the edge of a bridge. Bad luck.'

'In isolation, yes. But –'

Persistent bad luck had a cause. The stubborn attentions of a misfortune-bearing spirit, for example. Fox or tanuki mischief. Sometimes humans became the target of furious hatred for offences they did not even realize they were committing.

Kogetsu carefully unsealed a fraction of his

ayakashi powers – keeping enough in reserve that his ears and tail stayed hidden – and probed the space around Akifumi.

'But this is –'

He suddenly felt dizzy. His eyes narrowed of their own accord as a grim cast came over his face.

'What is it, Kogetsu? You don't look well, either.'

'I must be going,' Kogetsu said. Unable to look Akifumi in the face, he had already turned his back.

'Oh. Well, sorry to bother you with this. This leg'll be good as new in no time, and then we can start your lessons again.'

'Very well.'

Kogetsu left via the same window he had climbed in through, made himself invisible again, and left the property.

As he made his way back down Gloaming Lane, Kogetsu brooded on what he had seen.

Akifumi's existence had become so unstable that his grip on life itself was slipping. The man was half-dead already, drifting towards the other shore. And so –

'No wonder death is seeking to draw him nearer!'

Frustrated and furious, Kogetsu punched a

nearby wall. A tanuki girl watching from the shadows scampered off in fright.

He hadn't known. Hadn't known that humans in a precarious state, if left to their own devices, would drift inexorably towards the beyond.

Kogetsu cursed himself for failing to notice earlier. Now, without intervention, Akifumi would soon die.

But to prevent this, Kogetsu needed to know what had destabilized him, so he could remove the cause of his anxiety.

'What a tiresome development,' he muttered.

Furthermore, it would be foolish to assume that Akifumi was safe in his current situation. Dangers lurked within any household, and even if his leg healed Akifumi was liable to trip and hit his head on a table, or choke to death on mochi.

If Akifumi was to be saved, there was no time to lose.

From that day on, Kogetsu slipped invisibly into the Kohakuya household every day to eavesdrop on conversations among its residents, both family members and staff. He could have asked Akifumi directly what had put him in his predicament, but it seemed likely that the man himself did not know. Nevertheless, Kogetsu reasoned, he might be able to discern some clues from fragments of conversations between those who knew Akifumi.

His suspicion proved correct. From listening to the store's staff, he determined that, in fact, Akifumi had hoped to inherit the store from his father before this dream had been dashed.

Akifumi had always been a more skilled confectioner than his older brother, and so his brother had decided to have Akifumi take over the store while he entered another trade entirely, taking an apprenticeship in another household.

But his brother never managed to find his place in that household. He came back angry and resentful, insisting that, as the oldest son, he ought to inherit the Kohakuya after all.

The conflict-averse Akifumi had accepted this. He would be happy, he said, to support his brother as a confectioner in the store's kitchen.

'Clinging to wealth and fame and accumulating property always leads to such things,' Kogetsu sighed, once he grasped the extent of the battle over succession. 'Human greed runs deep.'

But it was not a lust for wealth or fame that made Akifumi want to inherit the Kohakuya. It seemed that, once his older brother gained control, he moved from managing the store as a whole to imposing his opinions about even the types of sweets that should be on display. Akifumi and the other confectioners were no longer free to pursue their craft as they pleased.

Kogetsu thought on the delight Akifumi had seemingly taken in teaching him the confectioner's art.

Perhaps he had volunteered to do this as a way of dealing with his frustration at not being able to create freely at the Kohakuya.

What Kogetsu needed was some way to draw out Akifumi's true feelings.

He was mulling this over as he roamed invisibly through the Kohakuya one day, when his eyes lit upon the chestnut *monaka*.

Of course! He could channel his *ayakashi* powers into sweets to give them the desired effects. Kogetsu was a *han-yo*, so his powers were weak and limited, but combining them with confections in a meaningful way might increase their potency.

A chestnut *monaka* would be the perfect vessel for an effect that drew out one's true feelings. The chestnut could stay hidden, but the truth had to come out: an amusing opposition.

Looking around at the other sweets on display, several other ideas came to Kogetsu. He decided to go home and start working immediately.

It would be his first attempt at creating sweets from start to finish without any guidance from Akifumi, but he was confident he could do it. After all, from winter through to early summer, he had eaten nothing but the sweets they had made together.

'Kogetsu! You're here to see me again?'

Some days later, Kogetsu came to Akifumi's room bearing the fruits of his labour. He entered through the window, of course. Akifumi was startled, but at the sight of his friend he smiled broadly.

Kogetsu looked around the room. The only thing that had changed since his last visit were the nightclothes Akifumi wore. Everything else, including the bandages on Akifumi's leg and the sling elevating it, was exactly the same. It was clear Akifumi could not take care of himself incapacitated like this, but presumably meals and changes of clothes were handled by the staff.

'I am,' Kogetsu said. 'And today I brought a proper gift.' He handed Akifumi a box.

Removing the lid, Akifumi saw a chestnut *monaka* and a *mame daifuku* inside.

'*Wagashi!*' he cried, delighted. 'You made these yourself? Even the *anko*?'

'Yes,' Kogetsu said. 'It took some time, I must admit.'

'Incredible!' Akifumi said, admiring Kogetsu's creations. 'These sweets look beautiful. They're perfect! I'd say you can hang out your shingle whenever you like. You must be some kind of prodigy to make a fully fledged confectioner out of yourself so quickly!'

'I had an excellent teacher,' Kogetsu said.

Akifumi was amazed. 'Why are you so indulgent today? Where are the usual cutting remarks?'

'Hurry up and try the sweets, please,' Kogetsu said. 'Start with the chestnut *monaka*.'

'You don't have to tell me twice!'

Kogetsu watched as Akifumi raised the *monaka* to his mouth and took a big bite.

'Delicious!' Akifumi said around a mouthful of sweet beans. After removing half of the *monaka* with his first bite, he was enjoying the second half in a more leisurely way.

Kogetsu sensed his own *ayakashi* powers radiating subtly from Akifumi. His plan had worked. Now he only needed to arrange the right situation.

'Akifumi,' he said. 'Do you have any feelings that you keep to yourself rather than sharing with those around you?'

'Who, me?'

'I'm sure you do. Think carefully.'

The confusion in Akifumi's eyes evaporated. Instead, he seemed to be gazing thoughtfully into the distance. And then, rapidly, as if feverish, he began to speak.

'I do, of course,' he said. 'I was pretending not to notice, but . . . I want to make *wagashi* my way. I want the freedom to think up new products and make special seasonal creations. I have so many ideas. I just need my brother's approval.'

Akifumi fell silent, gazing down at his hands uncertainly.

'Surely,' Kogetsu said gently, 'there are other paths open to you that do not require your brother's approval? Other ways to reach the freedom you seek?'

'Yes,' Akifumi said. 'You're right . . . Instead of working for my brother, I could strike out on my own and start my own store. Why didn't I ever think of that . . . ?'

His dreamy eyes came into focus and gleamed with hope.

'I wouldn't have the Kohakuya's clientele, or its history. Starting from nothing wouldn't be easy – but that's what would make it worth doing. It would be my store, so I could run it the way I'd want to.'

'All this time you have lived safely in the bosom of your family,' Kogetsu said. 'However, I believe you will prove more than capable in a harsh environment, too.'

Hearing his own true feelings slip from his mouth, Kogetsu realized that, for all his grumbling, he had great respect for this man.

'Kogetsu . . .' said Akifumi. 'Thank you. I feel

like eating this *monaka* helped me recover who I am.'

Akifumi's soul was no longer drifting towards the other shore. But Kogetsu could sense that his existence had not yet stabilized.

'I suspected as much,' Kogetsu murmured, biting his lip.

He had predicted that drawing out Akifumi's concerns and dispelling his reservations would not suffice to truly resolve the matter. Akifumi had visited Gloaming Lane almost every day, involving himself so deeply with Kogetsu that their fates had become intertwined. If their bond was not cut completely, Akifumi's unstable spirit would once again begin inching towards the otherworld.

Which was why Kogetsu had made the other confection in the box. He would have preferred not to use it, but he saw no other choice. He sighed.

'Akifumi,' he said. 'Won't you try the *mame daifuku*, too?'

'Try and stop me,' Akifumi said. 'I've been looking forward to this.' He took a bite, then said blissfully, 'Mm! This one's good, too. Perfect balance of sugar and salt.'

But then his expression went blank. He looked dazed, as if he was no longer even sure why he was eating the confection in his hand.

'Pardon me,' he said to Kogetsu, 'but who are you?'

Embarrassment, with a hint of suspicion. The ready smile and friendly tone of the preceding moments were gone.

Kogetsu forced his mouth into a smile of his own.

'Merely a visitor,' Kogetsu said. 'This house is so large that I lost my way and ended up in this room by accident.'

'Ah, of course.' Akifumi was visibly relieved. 'Let me call someone to help you find –'

'No need for that,' Kogetsu said, his palm firmly raised. 'I was just leaving.'

He turned and walked towards the door. As he put his hand on the doorknob, he turned back as if forgetting something.

'May I say one last thing, Akifumi?'

'By all means.'

'Farewell. You must never go back to that place again.'

Kogetsu closed Akifumi's door behind him, severing the bond between them for good. In the hall outside, he permitted himself a self-deprecating chuckle.

'A confection that makes you forget the person closest to you when you taste it. Quite perverse, if I say so myself. There are so many beans on the outside of a *mame daifuku*, however – who would notice if one were missing?'

And what was Kogetsu to Akifumi, if not a mere bean in the grand scheme of things? Their association had been a lark of a few months and no longer. Akifumi would not need Kogetsu to find success in his new business and create joy in life. Most importantly, he would live out his full, allotted span of years.

'A human life is the merest of moments, but I hope that it brings you happiness and contentment nonetheless.'

And with those words, Kogetsu vanished from the Kohakuya.

*

At his window beneath the new moon, Kogetsu kept his eyes closed for some time after this extended reverie was over.

Japan had changed much since then. There had been times of war, when instability and precarity had prevailed across the country, but now peace reigned. Of course, every age was home to some who found themselves destabilized by doubt and anxiety.

Word had reached Kogetsu's ears that Akifumi had founded his confectionery, far away, and made it a success.

Meanwhile, having learned that sweets enhanced with his *ayakashi* power could bring healing to the precarious and unstable, Kogetsu had opened the Amberglow Candy Store on Gloaming Lane.

He made a point of recommending confections best suited to addressing the issues of those who made their way to him, but this alone would have held little interest for him – too much like charity – and so he had begun collecting samples of emotions, too.

This was not simply because of Akifumi's warning that his lack of emotion would hinder his attempts at customer service. More importantly,

Kogetsu believed that understanding human emotions would also help him figure out why Akifumi had done what he'd done for him.

Why had he called Kogetsu a friend? Why had he gone to the trouble of teaching Kogetsu to make confectionery, and why had he brought him *okayu* on the full and new moon? Above all, why had Kogetsu himself felt the urge to save Akifumi?

All this had initially mystified him. But now, he felt a glimmer of comprehension.

Kogetsu rose to his feet and left his bedroom.

He walked into the hall, where a tall open cabinet stood directly behind the storefront's counter.

Kogetsu picked up one of the glass jars that filled the cabinet's shelves.

'A sample from that chestnut *monaka* incident,' he mused. 'The very confection that I fed to him.'

Every so often, Kogetsu came to this cabinet, took a jar in his hand, and partook in human emotion. In this way, over time, he had become more comfortable dealing with customers.

'This collection is growing quite extensive. I'll need to put it in order at some point. Relabel the jars, arrange them by year . . . How very tiresome.'

Some of the customers he saved had mistaken Kogetsu for a kami. And some had returned to the shrine to convey their gratitude.

However –

'I did not open the Amberglow Candy Store to save anyone. Those seeking such fine motives will find none of them here. It was simply a way to pass the time. Visitors would do well to remember that . . .'

Glossary

amazake

Literally 'sweet sake', this is made from rice using a similar process to actual sake but ends up much sweeter and whiter, and with a very low (or even zero) alcohol content. Often served hot at shrines during New Year's celebrations.

anko

Sweetened bean paste used in a huge range of *wagashi*. Most commonly made with red azuki beans. Types of *anko* include *koshi-an* (literally 'strained' *anko*, with a smoother texture), *tsubu-an* ('lumpy' *anko*, with bean fragments included for texture) and *shiro-an* ('white' *anko*, made from white beans instead of azuki).

ayakashi

Another word for a *yokai*: a mysterious, supernatural

being that lives just out of sight of humanity. A huge and diverse category, which includes everything from well-known creatures like the river-dwelling *kappa* to animated parasols . . . and foxes with eerie powers.

caramels
Chewy brown candies made by boiling sugars and mixing them with cream and butter.

candy apples / toffee apples
Apples on sticks with a brittle candy coating. In Japan, the same technique is used to make 'candy grapes', 'candy strawberries' and more.

daifuku
A small, soft mochi with a sweet filling, often *anko*.

kanoko
Short for *kanoko-mochi*. A ball of mochi or *yokan* coated in *anko* that is, in turn, studded with sweetened beans. *Kanoko* literally means 'deer fawn', and refers to the sweet's spotted appearance.

konpeito
Tiny, colourful sugar candies shaped like stars. The word *konpeito* comes from the Portuguese *confeito* (related to comfit in English), revealing that this type of sweet was first brought to Japan by Portuguese traders in the sixteenth century.

mame daifuku
A *daifuku* with whole beans (*mame*) embedded in the mochi and/or filling.

mame kanoko
A kind of *kanoko* which has many different kinds of beans in its outer layer, giving it an even more lively appearance.

manju
A small steamed bun with a sweet filling, usually *anko*. Often enjoyed at onsen.

monaka
A wafer shell filled with a sweet filling, usually *anko*. Some *monaka* are made with simple flat wafers rather than a shell, and look more like a sandwich.

neriame

A very sweet and viscous syrup eaten after being twisted and kneaded with chopsticks. *Neriame* is a kind of *dagashi*: cheap and cheerful sweets meant for kids to enjoy.

nerikiri

A mixture of *shiro-an* (sweet white bean paste) and glutinous rice flour. It can be moulded and cut into many different forms, so confectioners often use it as a medium for demonstrating their art, some even performing live demonstrations of the 'sculpting' process. *Nerikiri* shaped into seasonal motifs is particularly popular.

okayu

A kind of rice porridge, usually with something mixed in for flavour or texture. In Japan, *okayu* is the food traditionally served to invalids unable to eat regular steamed rice.

wagashi

Traditional Japanese sweets, as opposed to those from Europe and America, which are called *yogashi*.

'Traditional' is an accommodating category, though, and some kinds of *wagashi* were originally brought from overseas.

wasanbon
Delicate sweets made from a kind of sugar produced in Shikoku (the original meaning of *wasanbon*). The sugar is tinted with food colouring and pressed into moulds to create a range of shapes, including flowers, animals and geometric designs.

yokan
A mixture of *anko*, sugar and agar, sometimes studded with beans. It sets as a dense block that can be eaten in slices. Made in many other flavours, including matcha and even chocolate.

The Amberglow Candy Store

The Amberglow Candy Store

HIYOKO KURISU

Translated by Matt Treyvaud

MICHAEL JOSEPH

PENGUIN MICHAEL JOSEPH

UK | USA | Canada | Ireland | Australia
India | New Zealand | South Africa

Penguin Michael Joseph is part of the Penguin Random House group of companies
whose addresses can be found at global.penguinrandomhouse.com

Penguin Random House UK,
One Embassy Gardens, 8 Viaduct Gardens, London SW11 7BW

penguin.co.uk

Penguin
Random House
UK

First published in Japan in 2022 by Poplar Publishing Co., Ltd.
English language translation rights arranged with Poplar Publishing Co., Ltd. through
The English Agency (Japan) Ltd. and New River Literary Ltd.
First published in the UK by Penguin Michael Joseph in 2025

002

Originally published in Japanese as *Yuyamidori Shotengai – Kohaku Yogashiten*
Copyright © Hiyoko Kurisu, 2022
All rights reserved
English translation copyright © Matt Treyvaud, 2025

The moral right of the author has been asserted

No part of this book may be used or reproduced in any manner for the
purpose of training artificial intelligence technologies or systems. In accordance
with Article 4(3) of the DSM Directive 2019/790, Penguin Random House
expressly reserves this work from the text and data mining exception

Set in 13.5/17pt Dante MT Pro
Typeset by Falcon Oast Graphic Art Ltd
Printed and bound in Great Britain by Clays Ltd, Elcograf S.p.A.

The authorized representative in the EEA is Penguin Random House Ireland,
Morrison Chambers, 32 Nassau Street, Dublin D02 YH68

A CIP catalogue record for this book is available from the British Library

ISBN: 978–0–241–73345–5

Penguin Random House is committed to a sustainable future
for our business, our readers and our planet. This book is made from
Forest Stewardship Council® certified paper

MIX
Paper | Supporting
responsible forestry
FSC® C018179

Contents